"Hey!" Don called from one of the other rooms. "Hey, you guys, you'd better come back here!"

The two policemen, responding to the janitor's call, hurried toward him. When they reached the end of the hallway, they saw Don standing by an open door, looking into one of the offices.

"What is it?" Bill asked.

"It's Dr. Shaw," Don said, pointing.

When the two officers reached the door, they could see Dr. Shaw in his chair, his face down on the desk.

"Dr. Shaw?" Bill called. He walked over to the desk and raised Shaw up. The front of Shaw's shirt was covered with blood, and the doctor was obviously dead.

"You'd better call the station, Charley," Bill said. "I'd say this is a little more than vandalism, or even protest . . . ."

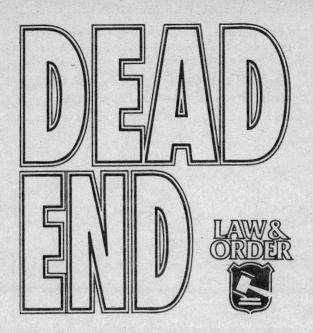

DEAD END

LAW & ORDER

A novel by Jack Gregory
based on the Universal television series
LAW AND ORDER
created by
Dick Wolf

ST. MARTIN'S PAPERBACKS

Published by arrangement with MCA Publishing Rights, a Division of MCA Inc.

LAW AND ORDER: DEAD END

Copyright © 1994 by MCA Publishing Rights, a Division of MCA Inc.

Front cover photograph courtesy The Stock Market.

ISBN: 0-312-92575-1

Printed in the United States of America

St. Martin's Paperbacks edition/May 1994

10 9 8 7 6 5 4 3 2 1

Chapter One

Manhattan, early October 7:00 A.M.

The deli on the corner was doing a brisk business in bagels and coffee as the city began another day. The morning commuter buses inched through the crowded streets with engines clacking, keeping their vehicles nose to tail to prevent any upstart motorist from cutting into the line. Yellow taxis changed lanes frequently and honked impatiently at pedestrians who insisted upon crossing without regard to the light or traffic.

A white van worked its way through the morning rush. On the side of the van was the cartoon rendering of a smiling bee, lifting a mop from a pail. The logo read: BUSY BEE CLEANING SERVICE.

The van stopped in front of Humaricare Medical Services, parking in a spot marked *For Staff Only*. Two men got.

"The Jets will disappoint you ever' time. I don't know why I even bother," the younger of the two was saying as he lifted down a large, white container on wheels. "I mean I must be some kind of nut to still like 'em, but what can I say? I got hooked on 'em when I was a kid and Joe Namath was winnin' games."

The older of the two brought out a vacuum cleaner. "I been tryin' to tell you, the Giants are the team you should like. I been followin' them now for more'n thirty years. Sure, they let you down sometimes, but all in all I been pretty— Holy shit. Tony, look at that."

"Look at what?" the younger man asked, glancing up.

"The front window there. It's smashed all to hell."

Tony unlocked the door, then the two men went inside.

"What do you think, Don? What the hell's goin' on here?" Tony asked.

"I don't know, but I don't like this," Don replied. "I don't like it one little bit."

Tony pushed the door open slowly, then he and Don stepped cautiously into the building.

"Hello? Hello, anyone here? We're the janitorial service," Tony called.

"Holy—" Don started, then stopped. The reception room was a mess. File cabinet drawers were standing opened, and shredded papers were scattered all over the floor. On the wall there was a picture of a pregnant woman, holding a gun to her swollen abdomen. "If you must abort your baby, try this!" the writing on the photo said.

The two men looked around for a moment, then Tony walked over to pick up the phone.

"What are you doin'?"

"I'm callin' the cops," Tony said. "I ain't takin' the blame for this."

"Good idea. We ought to call Dr. Shaw too. I'll call him from the other phone."

The two men made their calls. Tony got through to the police, but Don hung up with the phone still unanswered.

"Couldn't get him?"

"No," Don said, shaking his head. "Maybe he's already on the way in. He gets here early sometimes."

"You want to try Dr. Corrigan?"

"What, you mean call the head man himself?" Don shook his head. "No. If the cops want him, they can call him." He picked up the phone. "I'll try Shaw one more time. Maybe he was just in the bathroom or somethin'."

Unsuccessful again, Don hung up the phone, then stepped outside to smoke a cigarette while he and his partner waited for the police officers to show up. They didn't have long to wait. A unit arrived within four minutes of the call.

"You the two men who called in the vandalism report?" one of the policemen asked as he and the driver got out of the car.

"Yeah, we called it," Don answered, butting his cigarette. "Go on inside and have a look around."

"What about the people who work here? They been notified?"

"No. We called Dr. Shaw, but we couldn't get him. I figure he ought to be here by now. He generally gets here before we leave."

"Why did you call Shaw instead of Corrigan? Dr. Corrigan is the one in charge," the older of the two policemen said. They stepped inside.

"I don't know," Don answered. "I guess it's because Shaw is about the only one we ever see. Corrigan seems sort of standoffish."

"Jeez, Bill, look at all the glass on the floor," the younger policeman said.

"Yeah," Bill answered. "My guess is that it's protesters."

"Protesters? Why would anyone protest a doctor's office?"

Bill pointed to the picture of the pregnant woman. "Doesn't that give you an idea?"

"Oh. Abortion clinic, huh?"

"Not really. They don't actually do abortions

6

here. I think they do research on how abortions are done, or something.''

"Hey!" Don called from one of the other rooms. "Hey, you guys, you'd better come back here!"

The two policemen, responding to the janitor's call, hurried toward him. When they reached the end of the hallway, they saw Don standing by an open door, looking into one of the offices.

"What is it?" Bill asked.

"It's Dr. Shaw," Don said, pointing.

When the two officers reached the door, they could see Dr. Shaw in his chair, his face down on the desk.

"Dr. Shaw?" Bill called. He walked over to the desk and raised Shaw up. The front of Shaw's shirt was covered with blood, and the doctor was obviously dead.

"Oh, shit," the younger policeman said.

"You'd better call the station, Charley," Bill said. "I'd say this is a little more than vandalism, or even protest."

"Hey, Bill, look at that," Charley said, pointing to a pad beside Shaw. "He was trying to write something."

"T-A," Bill read, looking at the pad. He sighed. "Whatever it was he was trying to write, he didn't get it finished."

* * *

When Sergeant Lennie Briscoe and Detective Mike Logan arrived on the scene somewhat later, they saw vans from at least two television stations already there, as well as reporters for the print media. There were also several protesters milling around outside, many carrying signs that read: LET THE UNBORN LIVE! Others read, ACTION COMMITTEE FOR LIFE WATCH, or ACLW.

"What is all this?" Briscoe asked. "Why so much interest?"

"You haven't heard anything about Humaricare?" Logan replied.

"No, not really."

"They're a research outfit, working on an abortion pill."

"An abortion pill?"

"Yeah. Like the one they've got in France, only this one is supposed to be better."

"Build a better mouse trap," Briscoe mused. He nodded toward the group of demonstrators. "Only I don't think this is the world they wanted beating a path to their door."

The two detectives ran the gauntlet of news reporters and photographers to get inside the clinic. One of the uniforms recognized them and opened a path for them back to the office where the body had been found.

"How long?" Logan asked the M.E.

"From two to ten hours."

"In other words, it could've been just about anytime during the night?"

"That's about it."

"Thanks a lot," Logan said sarcastically.

"Glad to be of help. You want a rundown?"

"Yeah, let me hear it."

"Death by gunshot wound to the heart. I haven't extracted the bullet yet, so I can't give you a caliber. It was fired from very close, though. There are powder burns on the shirt."

"How long would it take a wound like that to kill?" Briscoe asked.

"Oh, death would be nearly instantaneous, I would think."

Briscoe pointed to the pad, and the pen, still in the deceased's hands.

"Would he have time to write a note?"

"No, not at all," the M.E. replied. He looked at the pad. "I'm surprised he was able to write that much."

"Do you think maybe he didn't?"

"I couldn't say. I don't think I could testify, absolutely, that he didn't. I'm just surprised that he did, that's all."

"Oh, Gary, no! No!" a woman called from the doorway. Logan and Briscoe turned and saw an attractive woman, in her late thirties or early forties. She wore a white lab coat with a little golden name tag over her left pocket. The tag read: DR. KASABIAN. Crying, the woman turned away and started toward the front of the building.

"Dr. Kasabian," Briscoe said to Logan. "That name mean anything to you?"

"No," Logan admitted. "I can't say that it does."

"How about it, can I move the body?" the M.E. asked.

"Yeah, we've seen enough," Briscoe replied. "Get plenty of pictures."

"I always get plenty of pictures," the M.E. grumbled.

Logan and Briscoe returned to the front of the clinic, where Dr. Kasabian was sitting on a sofa. Her eyes were red-rimmed and wet, and she held a tissue in one hand. Someone handed her a glass of water. A gray-haired man, wearing horn-rim glasses, was sitting at a computer terminal, tapping rapidly on the keys and looking at the screen in consternation.

"Excuse me, sir. What are you doing?" Logan asked the man.

"Gone! It's all gone! Everything! All our work!" the man said.

"Who are you?"

The man stood up, looked at Logan and Briscoe, then stuck his hand out. "My name is Corrigan. Dr. David Corrigan. I'm the staff director for Humaricare Clinic. Are you gentlemen from homicide?"

"Yes. I'm Logan, he's Sergeant Briscoe."

"I'm glad you're here. They've gone too far this time."

"They? Who are they?"

"The demonstrators. You saw them outside, didn't you? They're the ones responsible for this."

"It doesn't seem likely, does it, Doctor?" Logan asked.

"What do you mean?"

"I mean it doesn't seem likely that they would kill Dr. Shaw and then still be here, hanging around, when the police arrive."

"You can't gauge them by ordinary standards," Dr. Corrigan said. "They're crazy people, all of them. You remember what happened down in Pensacola, and out in Wichita. The kooks are waging open attacks on abortion clinics. It's getting to the point where being a doctor is a high-risk occupation . . . like being a police officer, or a coal miner."

Briscoe looked over at Dr. Kasabian, who was still crying quietly.

"Dr. Kasabian seems quite distraught, doesn't she?"

"She has every right to be. She and Dr. Shaw worked very closely. We all did, in fact, from the researchers all the way down to the lab technicians. His loss is going to be keenly felt around here, I can tell you that." Corrigan sighed, then looked back at the computer terminal. "Even more so since the murderers also destroyed the computer files. Dr. Shaw won't be around to help us reassemble the information."

"What information?" Logan asked.

"The research data on the PEBC. I'm afraid that whoever murdered poor Gary also infected the computers with a virus. Look."

Dr. Corrigan struck a few keys, then words began to flow across the screen. *Let the unborn live,* the message on the screen said.

"No matter which file I open, I get this message," Corrigan said, demonstrating by changing files.

"Do you have backup disks?" Logan asked.

"Backup disks? If you mean backup floppies, no."

"Excuse me, Doctor, I'm not very computer literate," Briscoe said. "But even I know you should keep backup disks."

"Well, of course we have our data backed up," Corrigan said. "Only it's not on floppy disks the way you might back up a household budget program. The information is on auxiliary hard-drive disks. But unfortunately they too are on-line with the primary system, and thus have been affected by the virus as well." Corrigan sighed. "I'm afraid we have nothing now."

"What about hard copy? Notebooks? That sort of thing?" Briscoe asked.

Dr. Corrigan shook his head. "Detective, in the field of research, we have top-secret clearance that is every bit as exclusive as that maintained by the government. We have a requirement that all hard-copy and handwritten data be destroyed, daily. We don't intend to lose the edge by letting someone clean out our waste baskets. PEBC is much too important for that."

"PEBC," Briscoe said. "What is that?"

"Post-event birth control," Corrigan replied.

"Birth control? You're getting this kind of reaction from working on a birth control pill?"

"Post-event birth control," Corrigan replied.

"Oh for God's sake, David, why don't you tell them what it really is?" Dr. Kasabian said. She got up from the couch and walked over to join the men. "I'm sorry about that little episode there. Gary was a very dear friend, in addition to being a colleague."

"Quite understandable, Doctor," Briscoe said. "What do you mean, 'tell them what it really is'?"

"It's a pill you can take on the morning after. That makes it an abortion pill. It's as simple as that," Kasabian said. "You have to understand that, technically, conception takes place as soon as the sperm reaches the egg. What our pill does, or rather will do, if we get it developed, will be to kill the embryo thus formed."

"Then it is abortion?"

"Certainly it isn't abortion to the degree of removing a developing fetus," Dr. Corrigan said. "That is why I believe calling it a post-event birth control pill is a more accurate way of expressing it."

"You are dealing in semantics, Doctor," Dr. Kasabian retorted. "For heaven's sake, I have nothing against abortion. I think it should be every woman's right to choose. But calling this a birth control pill is resorting to euphemism in order to make it more attractive, and thus more profitable. You hope to be able to attract women who have nothing against birth control, but who are put off by abortion."

"Yes, but I think even those people would be less apprehensive about it if they knew they were aborting a divided cell, rather than a human fetus."

"So when does human life begin, Doctor?" Dr. Kasabian asked.

"We haven't yet made that determination," Dr. Corrigan replied.

"Precisely. So until we do, let's call a spade a spade."

"Or, in this case, abortion an abortion," Logan suggested.

"Yes," Kasabian said. "And as I said, I have no problem with that. Abortion is legal and I believe it should stay legal. All we are attempting to do is make it easier, less traumatic, and much more affordable."

Two men came through the reception area then, pushing a gurney. On the gurney, covered by a green sheet, lay the body of Dr. Gary Shaw.

"I'll have pathology for you by late this afternoon," the M.E. said.

"Thanks, Doc," Briscoe replied.

Logan and Briscoe walked over to the front door of the clinic to watch the body being loaded onto the police hearse. There was a sizable crowd gathered outside, mostly the curious, but several were carrying anti-abortion signs.

There were also several TV cameras in operation, and almost before he knew it, Briscoe found a microphone shoved into his face. An attractive black woman was on the other side of the mike.

"Detective, is this another example of protest by terror? Are the anti-abortion activists going to continue to pursue their agenda by murdering physicians?"

"It's too early to make any such judgments about this case," Briscoe replied.

"But doesn't this warrant a comparison with the murder in Pensacola, and the shooting out in Wichita? Haven't the pro-lifers moved their protest to a newer, more dangerous level?"

"In both of those incidents, the shooter committed the act in broad daylight and in front of witnesses, calling attention to the event. In this case the murder was done in the dark. And, as I said earlier, it is much too early to speculate."

"But surely you have formulated an opinion?" the newswoman insisted.

"Sergeant Briscoe can't comment, but I will," Dr. Corrigan said, and the TV cameras and reporters moved to him. "I hold the anti-abortion demonstrators accountable for Dr. Shaw's tragic death."

"And what makes you think that, Doctor?"

"You should see inside. It's a mess. Our records are destroyed, or scattered all over the place. And they left their calling card on the wall . . . their narrow-minded diatribe against the freedom of choice."

"Dr. Corrigan, there are thousands of active demonstrators for the pro-life cause. Could you narrow your suspicions down a little?"

"I ask you. Who is the head of Action Committee for Life Watch?"

"Are you referring to Jerry Talbot?"

"Of course I'm referring to Jerry Talbot. He has caused us difficulty before. Why is this any different?"

"Jerry Talbot has demonstrated before, Doctor, but he has never engaged in any violent activity," one of the reporters said.

"Yes, well, perhaps Mr. Talbot felt things weren't moving quickly enough for him."

When Corrigan returned to the building, the reporters moved back to Briscoe. "Will you be arresting Jerry Talbot?"

"I'm sorry, I'm not going to answer any more of your questions now," Briscoe said, holding up his hand. "When we have something, we'll let you know."

Briscoe and Logan went back inside the clinic, leaving the reporters to finish up their stories by adding their own speculation.

"Things must've been easier before there were so many reporters," Logan grumbled.

"There's never been a time when there weren't many reporters," Briscoe said. "Before TV there were newspapers."

"Maybe so, but they weren't as immediate. I wish we could pass a law that would keep them away from all homicide cases until they were closed."

"What? And abridge the freedom of the press?" Briscoe said sarcastically. He ran his hand through his hair. "What about this Talbot? What do we know about him?"

"He's been a very visible spokesman for the Life Watchers," Logan replied.

"Life Watchers?"

"That's how they refer to themselves. I think I'll go back outside and talk to a few of them."

"Yeah, that's probably a good idea," Briscoe agreed.

Logan left, and Briscoe resumed questioning Corrigan, as Dr. Kasabian sat nearby.

"Dr. Corrigan," Briscoe said, "have you, or any of your staff, ever had any personal run-ins with this man, Talbot?"

"Oh yes, a number of times," the doctor replied.

"In what way?"

Dr. Corrigan pointed outside. "To begin with, what about the pickets? We've had absolutely no peace from them, ever since they learned that we were close to developing the PEBC pill."

"That's their right."

"Yes, well, they aren't just picketing here. Last month they showed up at a stockholders' meeting, and, before that, they organized a nationwide fax campaign, sending more than ten thousand faxes of pictures of unborn fetuses to influential people in government, business, and the media as a protest against the PEBC."

"There is nothing illegal about that either."

"All right then, what about physical harassment?" Dr. Corrigan asked. "We have been physically harassed by them."

"Can you be more specific?"

"Tell him, Linda."

"It was nothing," Dr. Kasabian said. "It was probably just my imagination."

"It wasn't just your imagination. And you were certainly frightened enough. Tell him."

"You had a physical confrontation with the ACLW?"

"Not with the ACLW. With Jerry Talbot himself."

"What happened?"

"Dr. Shaw was working late one night when he thought he might be on to something interesting. He called me—"

"Called you where?"

"At my apartment. It was quite late, nearly eleven, and I was home."

"I'm sorry, please continue."

"As I said, Dr. Shaw asked me to come down, so I did. Just as I started inside, though, I sensed someone watching me."

"You sensed someone?"

"Yes. It was a very, very strong sensation. I called out, asking who was there, but no one replied. I started toward the front door, walking so fast I was nearly running. Then, just before I reached the front door I saw him."

"Talbot?"

"Yes. He appeared, almost from nowhere."

"What did he do?"

"He opened the door for me."

"That's it? He just opened the door?"

"He spoke to her," Dr. Corrigan said.

"What did he say?"

"He said," Dr. Kasabian replied, " 'Were you frightened, Doctor? You have the means of defending yourself. You can run, you can scream, you can fight back. But what about the unborn? How can they defend themselves from you and others like you?' "

"That's all there was to it? Did he threaten you in any way?"

"No," Dr. Kasabian said. "As I said, he just opened the door for me."

"But it was the way he opened the door, and the implied threat in his words," Dr. Corrigan insisted. "So, as soon as she told me about it the next day, I reported it to the police. But they did nothing, absolutely nothing." Dr. Corrigan said. "I may as well have not even called them."

"What could they do? He made no physical threat. He violated no law."

"What about stalking? Isn't there a law against stalking?" Dr. Corrigan asked.

"Had there been previous times where he suddenly appeared like that?"

"No, that was the only time," Dr. Kasabian said.

"One time does not a stalker make."

"Perhaps not," Dr. Corrigan said, "but you must admit that it was a rather disconcerting confrontation."

"David, really, there wasn't that much to it," Dr. Kasabian said. "I told you then, don't bother to call the police. But you insisted, and look what it got you."

"Maybe it availed me nothing," Dr. Corrigan agreed. "But at least I let it be known that I don't appreciate Mr. Talbot skulking around my staff members like that."

"If you two will excuse me, I'm going to join my partner in asking a few questions on the picket line. Someone may have seen something that will help us."

"You won't get anything from any of them," Dr. Corrigan said. "They're all Talbot's people. They're all going to take up for him. They'll probably even lie for him."

Logan was with a young woman when Briscoe joined him.

"Anything?" Briscoe asked.

"Nothing so far," Logan replied. "This is Mrs. Andersen."

"With an *e*," the woman said. "People always want to spell it with an *o*, but it's A-n-d-e-r-s-e-n."

"Mrs. Andersen, do you have any information that might be helpful?"

"I'm afraid not, officer. I think it's a terrible tragedy, but I didn't know anything about it until after I had already arrived this morning."

"If you didn't know what happened here, why did you come here today?"

"Well, because this was my day," Mrs. Andersen said.

"Excuse me. Your day? What do you mean by that?" Briscoe asked.

"Our chapter is divided into seven teams, one team for each day. Today was the day for our team. And, as I say, it wasn't until we got down here and saw the police and cameras that we knew something had happened."

"What about Talbot? Jerry Talbot? When is the last time you saw him?"

"I haven't seen him in almost a week," Mrs. Andersen said. "He generally comes down to the picket site at least once every day, to sort of give us encouragement. You aren't saying Jerry Talbot had anything to do with killing that doctor, are you?" she asked.

"We're not saying anything," Logan replied.

"Because if that's what you're implying, you're wrong—dead wrong. Why, Jerry Talbot is the most compassionate and caring human being I have ever met."

"I'm sure he is," Briscoe replied dryly.

Briscoe left Mrs. Andersen and interviewed several others. One of them was off by himself, away from the others. He identified himself as Paul Alfusco.

"Alfusco?" Briscoe said. The name seemed

to strike some sort of responsive chord, but he couldn't call it up.

"Paul Alfusco," the man said. He was short and stocky, with thinning gray hair.

"Mr. Alfusco, is there anything you can add to what went on here?"

Alfusco shook his head. "I'm sorry," he said. "I'm just a bystander."

"A bystander? Aren't you with these people?" Briscoe took in the demonstrators with a wave of his hand.

"Yes, I'm with them," Alfusco said. "I'm opposed to abortion and I'm here to demonstrate that opposition."

"This is your day?" Briscoe asked.

"Pardon?"

"One of the others said that you were broken down into teams, one team each day. This is your day?"

"Yes. This is my day. That's why I'm here, not because of anything that may have happened in the clinic last night. I know nothing of it. I certainly don't want anyone to think that murder is the way we send our message. I don't approve of such things."

"We agree on that," Briscoe said. He gave Alfusco his card. "If you hear anything, would you please give me a call?"

"Yes, I will," Alfusco promised.

Logan came up just as Briscoe was finishing

his interview with Alfusco. "Come up with anything interesting?" he asked.

"No," Briscoe replied. "How about you?"

"Nada."

"Let's go back inside and have another look around," Briscoe suggested. "Then we can go back to the station house and put together what we've got."

"Ha, that won't be a very long meeting," Logan said sarcastically. "So far we've got nothing."

Chapter Two

That's the place over there, Mike," Briscoe said, pointing through the windshield to a walk-up brownstone next door to a tobacco store.

Logan pulled the gray, unmarked Ford into a U-turn in the middle of the street, angering a taxi driver, who honked impatiently.

"Hey! Do you think you own the goddamned street, mister?" the hack shouted.

"Sorry," Logan called back. When he hooked both wheels up on the sidewalk in a no-parking zone, the cabby realized they must be police officers, and drove off without further comment.

"You ready?" Logan asked.

Briscoe checked his pistol, but didn't remove it. "Yeah," he said. Like Logan, he hung his badge folder from his jacket pocket. "Let's go."

The two men hurried up the foot-polished cement steps then through the door into the downstairs lobby. The lobby carpet was threadbare, stained, and smelly. The super, seeing them come in, hurried out of his office just off the lobby.

"Is there something I can help you gentlemen with?" he asked.

"Police," Logan said, turning so the super could see his badge. "You have a Jerry Talbot living here?"

"Yes, sir. He's on the third floor. Apartment 3D."

"Which one would that be?"

"That would be the second door on the right-hand side."

"Is he here now?" Briscoe asked.

"Well, I . . . I don't know, really. I haven't seen him go out today, but he may have left without my seeing."

"These stairs the only way up or down?"

"Yes, sir."

Logan and Briscoe hurried up the stairs, pulling their pistols out as they approached the third floor. On the landing, a woman carrying a small child walked toward them. She gasped when she saw the guns in their hands, and wrapped her arms around her child protectively.

Logan put his finger across his lips. "Police," he whispered, pointing to the badge hanging from his jacket pocket.

The woman nodded in understanding, though her eyes were still wide with fear.

"Go on down the stairs," Logan said.

Nodding, the woman hurried down the steps. When she was out of sight, Logan turned back to Briscoe and nodded.

With Briscoe leading the way, the two men moved down the hallway to the second door on the right. Then, as they stood on either side of the door, Briscoe knocked.

"Mr. Talbot?"

The door opened as far as the latch chain would allow.

"Yeah?"

"Are you Mr. Talbot? Jerry Talbot?" Briscoe asked.

"Who wants to know?"

"We're police officers, Mr. Talbot. We want to talk to you."

"Just a minute," Talbot said. He pushed the door shut as if he were going to release the chain. Instead they heard the latch turning, then the sound of something falling over.

"He's running!" Logan said.

"Go ahead," Briscoe said, nodding toward the door.

Logan stepped back and kicked the door just beside the door knob. On the second kick the door crashed open, and both policemen ran inside.

"There!" Briscoe said, pointing to the open window.

Logan was the first to the window, and when he leaned through it, he saw Talbot on the fire escape, already one floor below. "He's heading down!" Logan shouted, climbing through the window after him.

Briscoe turned and ran back out the door, then down the stairs, moving so quickly that he overtook the woman and her child just before reaching the lobby. He dashed by the startled super and pushed his way through the front door, then vaulted over the porch railing. He ran to the opening of the alley, reaching it just as Talbot approached.

"Freeze!" Briscoe shouted, leveling his pistol.

Talbot turned and ran the other way. Briscoe could have dropped him easily, but he didn't shoot. Instead, with a sigh of frustrated anger, he put his pistol away and gave chase. Logan popped out from the corner of the building in front of Briscoe.

"He went that way!" Briscoe shouted, pointing.

Logan started after him. When Briscoe rounded the corner a second later, he saw Talbot almost to the top of a high board fence at the end of the alley, with Logan right behind him.

"Hold it, Talbot! Hold it right there!" Logan shouted, aiming his own pistol. Like Briscoe, however, Logan chose not to shoot, and Talbot dropped down on the other side.

Logan reached the fence, then went up to the top. He paused there and looked around.

"Do you see him?" Briscoe called up.

"No," Logan replied. "I'm going over. Why don't you go on back to the car and cruise around looking for him? Pick me up over on Beeker."

Five minutes later Briscoe saw Logan leaning against the front of a building, breathing heavily.

"Didn't get a sight of him," Logan said as he slipped disgustedly into the passenger seat.

"Neither did I," Briscoe said. He sighed. "Well, do we go see Lieutenant Van Buren?"

"Yeah, it's somethin' I'm really looking forward to," Logan replied sarcastically.

"You didn't pick him up?" Lieutenant Van Buren asked. Anita Van Buren was an attractive woman. She had taken Captain Cragen's place. Van Buren was black, female, and younger than Lennie Briscoe. Of the three things, Briscoe personally had the most difficulty with the fact that she was younger than he was.

"We let him get away," Briscoe said.

"You let him get away," Van Buren repeated. It wasn't a question, it was merely a reinforcement of the two men's failure.

"It's my fault, Lieutenant. I should've gone around back just in case he tried something like this," Briscoe said.

"It's no more your fault than mine," Logan said.

Van Buren held up her hand. "Don't fall over each other taking the blame," she said. "The bottom line is he got away from you. From both of you. Now what are you going to do about it?"

"He can't stay out of sight forever," Logan said. "This guy has been a real publicity hound. His pictures are all over the place. We can put out a wanted on him pretty easily."

"Do it. By the way, the lab report is in. There's a copy on your desks."

"Thanks," Briscoe said.

Briscoe and Logan left Van Buren's office and returned to their desks, which butted against each other.

"Want some coffee?" Logan asked.

"Yeah, that would be nice," Briscoe said as he

opened the folder for the lab report. The first thing to meet his eyes was a photo of the victim. Dr. Shaw's nude body was lying on the autopsy table. There was a single bullet hole just inside of and about one and a half inches below the left nipple.

Logan brought two cups of coffee over and handed one to Briscoe.

"Thanks," Briscoe said. "Looks like a nine millimeter," he added, reading from the lab report.

"Nine millimeter? Not exactly your Saturday night special. Nine millimeter guns tend to be a little more expensive than your twenty-twos, thirty-twos, or thirty-eight, Saturday night specials. Here you go. This is what I've been looking for."

"What's that?"

"The poster on the wall? The one with the pregnant woman holding the gun to her stomach? They got a good match on prints. Talbot's prints."

"No wonder he ran when we came to talk to him," Logan said. "And don't forget the note Shaw left," he added. "Or what may have been a note. T-A . . . He had to mean Talbot."

"Yeah. Well, the truth is, that's bothering me just a little. I'm not sure he would have had time to write even that much."

"Come on, Lennie. I've heard of guys who

were shot through the heart getting off five or six shots of their own before they died.''

"Maybe so, but that's reflex action. I mean if the last conscious thought of your brain was to pull your trigger finger, the nerves and muscles could take over. But writing—even two letters— is a cognitive action. Uh-oh," Briscoe said.

"What is it?"

"Did you look at the fingerprint report? We've got a new player in the game."

"Yeah?"

"There's a very clear print on the front of Shaw's desk. And it isn't Talbot's."

"Maybe it's one of the employees. Someone could've just come in to talk to him and leaned on his desk."

"Maybe, but the same print was found on the torn-up files."

"Okay, so Talbot had someone with him."

"Yeah, looks like it," Briscoe agreed. "Well, that's good. It's harder for two people to keep a secret than it is for one. One of them is going to slip up."

The two men studied the reports for a few minutes longer, then Briscoe finished his coffee and set the mug down.

"Listen, what do you say we get a warrant, then go back out to Talbot's apartment building and have a look around his place?"

"Sound's like the sensible thing to do," Logan agreed.

"Bingo!" Logan said, three-quarters of an hour later, holding up a small box. They were in Talbot's apartment searching for the gun, or anything else that might be useful.

"What have you got?" Briscoe asked, looking over at him from a bookshelf.

Logan showed him a yellow and red box. "I have a box of shells," he said, smiling. "Nine millimeter shells," he added.

"Well, now, isn't that a nice coincidence?" Briscoe replied. "It sure would help if we could turn up the piece."

"And then get a ballistics match," Logan agreed. He sighed. "Let's keep looking. It has to be around here somewhere."

Half an hour later, however, he said, "It's nowhere. We've looked everywhere."

"I guess we couldn't have been lucky enough for it to still be here. He's ditched it by now," Briscoe said.

"As long as we're out here, you want to see if we can find him?" Logan suggested. "We could talk to a few people."

"Yeah, we may as well make the rounds," Briscoe agreed. "What is it they say? Good police work is ten percent inspiration and ninety percent perspiration?"

Logan laughed. "I think that was Edison talking about scientific research."

"Maybe so, but it fits," Briscoe insisted.

Elizabeth Harris lived across the hall. She was the same woman they had encountered on the landing when they came for Talbot earlier.

"I don't know why you're picking on him," she said. Her child was sitting in a high chair, and she was feeding him strained peas and carrots, using the spoon to catch the spillover from his lips, then giving it back to him. "I can't believe he would do anything wrong," she continued. "He is such a nice person . . . so caring. He couldn't have done what you say he did."

"Actually, we aren't saying he did anything, ma'am," Briscoe replied. "All we're trying to do is talk to him."

"I saw it on television. They're already accusing him of murdering Dr. Shaw. Well, I assure you, he didn't do it."

"Why are you so sure?" Logan asked. "Can you provide him with an alibi?"

"What do you mean?" Elizabeth asked, looking up from the feeding.

"I mean, he lives right across the hall from you. Can you personally vouch for his whereabouts for the entire night?"

"Are you suggesting that I'm sleeping with

him, officer?" Elizabeth asked sharply. "My being a single mother does not give you the justification to reach such a conclusion."

"I'm suggesting no such thing," Logan replied easily. "I just want to know if you have any concrete reason for believing that Talbot is innocent, that's all."

"I believe in his cause, that's reason enough," Elizabeth said. "I mean, look at me. I could have aborted little Timmy. I had no money and I was young, pregnant, and unmarried. But Jerry Talbot talked me out of abortion, and I'm glad he did. I can't imagine my life without Timmy now. All Jerry Talbot wants is for other women to appreciate that life is a gift. He is one of the innocent, and yet people like you, and those in the news media, insist upon persecuting him."

"If he's all that innocent, why did he run from us?" Logan asked.

"Who wouldn't run? I mean, you came up here with guns in your hands and you kicked in his door. I was here, remember? I saw you. I'm no fool, and neither is Mr. Talbot. All of America has seen the way policemen act when things don't go their way. A motorist in Los Angeles, a suspect in Detroit."

Briscoe sighed. "Look, Mrs.—"

"Miss," the woman corrected. "It is *Miss* Harris, not Mrs. I feel no shame in being an unwed mother . . . certainly less shame than you policemen should feel in brutalizing innocent people—kicking them when they're down, beating them with sticks and flashlights.''

"I will grant you, Miss Harris, there are always a few exceptions to the rule, but ninety-nine percent of the police officers, certainly of the ones that I know, are professional men and women who do not engage in beating their victims. Perhaps it would interest you to know that in all the years I've been a police officer, I have never had to hit anyone with a nightstick or a flashlight.''

"No, you just kick their doors in.''

"Do you know anything about Jerry Talbot?'' Logan asked. "Where he's from? Any relatives or close friends we might speak with?''

"I've told you all I know,'' Elizabeth insisted, sticking another spoonful of food into her baby's mouth.

"Yes. Well, thank you very much for your trouble,'' Briscoe said.

"Wait a minute,'' she called as they were leaving. "I can tell you this. He has a sister somewhere.''

"A sister? Where?''

"I don't know. I heard him mention her once, that's all.''

"Do you know her name?''

"No, I don't know that either. The only reason I told you this much is because I'm sure he's innocent, and if you find his sister and talk to her, maybe she can do a better job of convincing you than I have."

"Thank you, Miss Harris," Briscoe said.

One of the other tenants in the building also knew that Talbot had a sister somewhere, but, like Elizabeth Harris, was unable to come up with a name.

"What do you say we go back to the station and pull this guy's rap sheet?" Briscoe suggested after they had interviewed everyone in the apartment. "If we find any woman's name connected with him, mentioned more than once . . ."

"It might be his sister," Logan said, finishing the thought for him. "Good idea."

Briscoe smiled, broadly. "Yeah, well, there's the ten percent inspiration I was talking about."

Half an hour later the two officers were examining all the documentation regarding Jerry Talbot's previous arrests. He had been arrested six times, every arrest in regard to his continued and active protest of abortion.

"Here's a cute one," Briscoe said, reading from one report. "He once put a dead baby rabbit in a plastic bag of blood and saline solution, then threw it at a young sixteen-year-old girl and her older sister as they were walking toward an abortion clinic. The sixteen-year-old was pregnant and unmarried, but get this. The older sister was also pregnant, married, and had every intention of keeping her baby. However, she was so traumatized by the incident that she suffered a miscarriage."

"That's the 'nice guy' that everyone told us about?" Logan asked.

"Yeah. Ah, here you go. Mrs. Pauline Gray, 410 Central Park West. I picked her name up a while ago, but I wanted to be sure. Now, here it is again. She's made bond for him three times."

"Four times. I've got her here too. She has to be the sister," Logan said. He closed the folder and stood up. "What do you say we have a talk with her?"

Four ten Central Park West was one of many towering apartment buildings on the west side of Central Park, which overlooked the park itself. A uniformed doorman opened the door for Logan and Briscoe.

"Would you happen to know which apartment is Mrs. Pauline Gray's?" Logan asked.

"Is Mrs. Gray expecting you?"

"I wouldn't be surprised."

"Salesmen?"

"Police."

"Would you let me see a badge, please?"

Both officers showed their badge.

"Yes, okay. I do hope you gentlemen aren't offended that I asked, but the salesmen today, they'll try anything to get in, and of course, my job is to keep people like that away from all our tenants. Especially from Mrs. Gray. They torment her the most, poor soul."

"What makes Mrs. Gray so popular with salesmen?" Logan asked.

"You mean you gentlemen don't know who she is?"

Briscoe shook his head no.

"Why, she's Mrs. Pauline Gray, of Pauline's," the doorman said. When he saw that they still didn't recognize the name, he explained, "Pauline's are very fashionable, very expensive hair salons. Only the best people go there. Why, she has them all over New York."

"Yeah, now that I think about it, I have seen them," Logan said. "They have those pink signs out front, with the name Pauline's, written in purple script."

"Those are the ones," the doorman said. "And to think, when her husband died, she owned only the one shop. It just goes to show you what a determined woman can do today." Remembering then that the two men had introduced themselves as police officers, the doorman frowned. "I do hope you aren't here to make any trouble for her."

"What's her apartment number?" Briscoe

asked, without answering the doorman's implied question.

"Fifteen B. There's the elevator right back there." The doorman pointed to the rear of the broad lobby.

"Thanks."

Just before the doors closed on the elevator, Briscoe saw the doorman reaching for a phone.

"Our arrival will not be unexpected," he said.

Logan chuckled. "Maybe not, but I doubt that she'll jump out the window."

When the elevator doors opened on the fifteenth floor, a woman was already standing by the open door of Apartment B. She was wearing black, form-fitting pants and a blouse of gold silk. She was a very pretty woman, one of those who, through expensive creams, rinses, facials, and so forth, managed to hold back the signs of age. It was impossible to tell whether she was in her late thirties or early fifties. She was holding, and gently stroking, a Siamese cat.

"You are policemen?" she asked. Her soft, modulated voice seemed to fit her appearance.

"Yes, ma'am," Briscoe replied, showing his badge. "I'm Sergeant Briscoe, this is Detective Logan."

"I am Pauline Gray. I assume you are here to ask about my brother," the woman said. She stepped away from the door by way of invitation. "Won't you please come in?"

The apartment was in sharp contrast to Jerry Talbot's. It was large, exquisitely furnished, and tastefully decorated. Sunlight streamed in through windows that looked out over the park, but quietly humming air conditioners kept the apartment cool.

"Would you like some tea?" she invited, putting the cat down. Her body moved under the silk blouse, and Logan noticed not only that she was wearing nothing beneath the blouse, but that she was the kind who could get away with it.

"Thank you, no," Briscoe replied.

"I was just about to have some myself. You won't mind?"

"No, of course not."

"Please, sit down."

"Mrs. Gray, we don't intend to impose upon you that long," Briscoe said. "All we want is a little information about your brother."

"Yes, I assumed as much. However, that is not something I can give you in a brief moment. It will take a little explaining." She held her hand out toward the sofa. "Please, do have a seat. Let me explain."

Logan and Briscoe sat on the sofa. Mrs. Gray sat in a chair across from them and picked up a small, china teacup. Logan was intrigued with the mystery of the woman. He didn't know if she was younger or older than he was. If younger, then she was possessed of a surprising sense of self-assured calm. If older, she had found the secret of youth, for her skin was soft, clear, and smooth, and her eyes were bright and unlined.

"You have to understand my brother," the woman said, seemingly as unconscious of her attractiveness as a lithe teenager. "Buddy is very—"

"Excuse me. Who did you say?" Briscoe asked, interrupting her.

Mrs. Gray smiled. "But of course, you wouldn't recognize him by that name. I'm speaking of my brother, Jerry Talbot. When we were kids, everyone called him Buddy. I still do."

"I'm sorry. Please go on."

"Buddy and I are all that's left now," Mrs. Gray said. "Both of our parents are dead. My husband has passed away, and I have no children. We had a sister, an older sister, named Sharon. Sharon . . . well, the expression they used to use was 'got into trouble.' In those days the proper thing to do when a girl got into trouble was for the boy and girl to get married. Only Sharon couldn't marry the boy . . . because he wasn't a boy. He was a man . . . a pillar of society, and he was already married. He did do what was considered the next best thing,

I guess. He provided the money for an abortion. Only, abortions weren't legal then. So Sharon had to go to a sleazy hotel room where some quack doctor, who had long since lost his license to practice, performed the operation. I'm sure you've guessed the story by now. Infection set in, and Sharon died." Mrs. Gray punctuated her story with a swallow of tea.

"I don't understand," Logan said. "You would think your brother would be for legalized abortions because of that. I mean it was to prevent just such a thing that they were made legal in the first place. And this pill they're working on would make it even more safe."

"Oh, I quite agree with you, officer," Mrs. Gray said. "And I am for a woman's choice. But Buddy doesn't see it that way. He looks at the botched job and the resultant infection as merely the symptom of the disease. The disease, he believes, is abortion itself. Consequently he has been passionately opposed to abortion in any form. And that passion has led him to become most active in expressing his opposition."

"Just how far do you think that passion would take him?" Briscoe asked.

Mrs. Gray smiled and put her cup back on the saucer. "I do not believe he killed that doctor, if that's what you mean," she said. "He would not do such a thing."

"Maybe he didn't plan to. Maybe he didn't

know Dr. Shaw was there. When the doctor discovered him, he panicked," Logan said.

"No," Mrs. Gray said. She shook her head and smiled calmly. "No matter what scenario you paint for me, I will not believe that Buddy had anything to do with it. It's more than a belief, it is a conviction."

"We have to face some facts, Mrs. Gray. We have definite evidence that places your brother on the scene on the night of the murder. We also know that he wasn't alone. All right, maybe your brother didn't do it. Maybe it was the person who was with him."

"No, that's not true. Buddy didn't know anything at all about the murder until he saw the news of the murder on TV. That's when he became very frightened, because he knew that he would be a prime suspect."

"You have seen him since then?"

"I haven't seen him, but he did call me."

"Do you know where he is?"

"No, he didn't tell me."

"Do you have any idea where he might be?"

"I'm afraid not."

"You said he knew he would be a prime suspect. Why did he think that, did he tell you?"

"Yes, of course, but he didn't have to tell me. It was obvious that my brother, who has been very visible in his protest, would be a suspect."

"Will he come to see you?"

"I don't know. I doubt it. He isn't dumb, I'm certain he knows that my place will be watched."

"Mrs. Gray, if you have any idea where he might be, I urge you to tell us. And I ask you this for your brother's own good," Briscoe said. "His picture has already gone out over television and the wire services. I'm afraid that until we bring him in, he is in some degree of danger."

"Why would that put him in danger? Have you put out a 'Wanted, Dead or Alive' poster on him?"

"No," Briscoe said. "But I think you will find that there are as many passionate people on the other side of this question as there are on your brother's side. And one of them may take it in his or her mind to avenge Dr. Shaw's death in order to send a message to others who are like your brother."

"There is no one else like my brother, Sergeant Briscoe," Mrs. Gray said. She sighed. "However, if my brother contacts me again, I will urge him to turn himself in."

"I hope you do, Mrs. Gray. And, for his own sake, I hope he listens to you."

They left the apartment, then rode the elevator in relative silence down to the lobby. There, the doorman came over to speak with them.

"Did you have a nice visit with Mrs. Gray?" he asked solicitously.

"Yeah, well, your warning helped," Logan replied sarcastically.

"I'm sorry about that, but I have an obligation to our tenants," the doorman said.

"Listen, do you know Jerry Talbot, Mrs. Gray's brother?" Briscoe asked.

"I don't know him personally. I do recognize him when I see him. He comes to visit Mrs. Gray from time to time."

"Has he been here in the last few days?"

"No, sir, I don't believe so. I think it has been at least a week or so since I saw him last."

Briscoe handed the doorman his card. "If he comes again, I want you to call me, do you understand? The moment you see him, you call me."

"Please, officer, I'd rather not get involved in all this."

"You got yourself involved when you called upstairs to tell Mrs. Gray we were here," Briscoe said. "For all we know, her brother might have been there with her all the time we were. If you hadn't warned Mrs. Gray, we might have run into him. Your warning gave her time to hide him."

"He wasn't there."

"How do you know? He could've come in sometime when you weren't on duty."

"Yes, I . . . I suppose he could have."

"And if he was there and you warned him, that would put you right in the middle of all this, wouldn't it?"

"Oh dear," the doorman said. "Yes, I suppose so."

"Call me," Briscoe said again.

"Yes. Yes, I will do that," the doorman promised, slipping the card into his shirt pocket.

Chapter
Three

Claire Kincaid peeled the cellophane wrapping from a steaming microwave bowl of macaroni and cheese, blew on it a couple of times, then set it on the table. This would be her dinner, and now that she thought of it, her lunch as well, for she had been so immersed in court documents during the noon period that she didn't even leave her desk.

Claire was actually a good cook, and there were times when she enjoyed preparing a gourmet meal. But she was too busy, and too ambitious in her position as Assistant D.A., to take the time to cook. Besides, gourmet meals were only fun if there was someone to cook them for.

Claire picked up the remote and turned on

the TV set, then channel surfed through the talk shows, quiz shows, Spanish language shows, reruns of sitcoms and westerns until she found some local news.

"Dr. Corrigan said there is an alarming trend throughout the country toward violence as a means of expressing protest. He spoke with our Betina Blake," the anchor man said. His picture was replaced by that of Betina Blake, an attractive young, black woman, dressed in a pale pink suit. Betina was interviewing an older man, identified by the superimposed logo as: Dr. David Corrigan, Director, Humaricare Medical Research Group.

"We are seeing an emerging pattern here. Disgruntled employees lash out in anger by violence in the workplace. College professors gunned down by students who are upset with their grades. The time-honored art of peaceful protest has been swept by the wayside. Redress of grievances by petition, poster, broadside, and picket line, has been replaced by the pistol and the bomb. It should come as no surprise to anyone that Dr. Shaw was murdered. Anyone with half a mind could see that it was coming," Dr. Corrigan said.

"What about the police? Did you inform them of your concern?" Betina asked.

"Of course we did. Unfortunately, the demonstrators were breaking no law by merely protesting. Which means the police could do nothing . . . until it was too late. So, the police did nothing, and now Dr. Shaw

is dead. And the true tragedy here is the loss to the scientific and medical community. Dr. Shaw was one of the most brilliant researchers of our time . . . in the style of Salk and Sabine."

"Tell me, Dr. Corrigan, how close are you to developing an American version of the abortion pill developed in France?"

"Our project is radically different from the RU 486. We prefer to call ours a post-event birth control pill. If taken within forty-eight hours of conception, it causes a spontaneous cessation of development, allowing the fertilized egg to be passed out of the system naturally, just as if fertilization had never taken place.

"But isn't the definition of a spontaneous cessation, abortion?"

Dr. Corrigan smiled. *"Yes, of course it is, and I don't really intend to be playing semantics. But the term 'abortion' has grown into its own meaning, so that it has its own dictionary, its own set of values, defended or attacked according to the bent of one's politics. Therefore I like to leave it alone and stay with words that have not gone beyond their boundaries."*

"Do you have any messages for whoever did this?"

Dr. Corrigan looked into the camera. *"Yes, I do. To whoever murdered Dr. Shaw. I want you to realize the magnitude of what you have done. In your zeal to force unwanted babies to be born to troubled young women, you have, in effect, condemned thousands, perhaps hundreds of thousands, of people to die of diseases for which there is now no cure. A man with Dr. Shaw's intellect might well have discovered a cure for cancer, or heart disease, or, yes, even AIDS. You may well have changed history in a way that is horrible for mankind."*

Betina Baker looked feelingly into the camera to do the closure. *"Heartfelt words from a colleague and close, personal friend of Dr. Gary Shaw, found murdered today in the Humaricare Medical Research Clinic. Though no arrests have been made, the police are looking for Jerry Talbot, a known anti-abortion demonstrator. Anyone knowing Mr. Talbot's whereabouts are urged to contact the police immediately. Citizens are cautioned that Talbot might be armed and dangerous. Betina Baker, On-the-Spot News Team."*

When it returned to the studio, the anchor man put up a photograph of Jerry Talbot.

"Jerry Talbot is approximately five feet ten inches tall and weighs 155 pounds. He has light brown hair, blue eyes, and a small scar on his chin. Anyone knowing his whereabouts is urged to contact the police immediately. Do not attempt to apprehend him yourself. I repeat, do not attempt to apprehend him yourself, as he may be armed, and he may be dangerous."

"In other news, the city can expect to experience some acute traffic problems tomorrow when—"

Claire turned the TV off in mid-sentence, then called Assistant D.A. Benjamin Stone.

Stone was stretched out on the sofa in his study, reading a novel. The Moody Blues were playing on the stereo, and a cool drink was on the table beside him. When he heard the ring, he dropped the paperback book across his chest and reached for the little cordless phone.

"Stone."

"Ben, this is Claire. Have you been watching the news?" Claire asked in the almost breathless enthusiasm that had come to be her signature.

"I try to avoid the news, Claire. It depresses me."

"You mean you haven't heard about the murder of that medical research doctor?"

"Are you talking about the doctor at the abortion clinic? Yes, of course I've heard about it."

"Humaricare isn't an abortion clinic," Claire insisted. "It is a medical research facility."

"But they are working on an abortion pill, right?"

"Among other things, yes," Claire agreed.

"What about it?"

"That's my kind of case, Ben. I want us to have it."

"Wait a minute, Claire. Am I missing something here? Has an arrest been made? Have charges been filed?"

"No, not yet. But it's just a matter of time. And when it happens, I want you to ask Wentworth to give it to us."

"If we draw it, fine, but I'm not going to Wentworth and ask that he assign it to us."

"Why not, Ben? It's going to be a very high-profile case."

Ben chuckled. "And that's what you want? A high-profile case?"

"Of course. And don't you see? It would be a perfect case for us. Your experience and my passion. I really want to put that guy away."

"Put who away?"

"Talbot. You know, the person who shot Dr. Shaw."

"We don't know that Talbot did do it."

"You're right, I'm jumping the gun. But whoever did it, when they arrest him—or her—and bring that person in, I want to send a message, loud and clear, that we won't tolerate the kind of things here that are going on in other parts of the country."

"Claire, if you want to send messages, get into the communications business. We're in the legal business, remember?"

"The two are not necessarily incompatible, Benjamin."

"You know your problem, Claire? You lack intensity," Ben said, chuckling. "I'll see you tomorrow."

Laughing at his sign-off, Claire hung up the phone then returned to her macaroni and cheese, now grown cold. She debated with herself whether or not to return it to the microwave, then decided to take it as it was. She turned the TV on again.

Humaricare lab, next day

Dr. Victor Trailins, a researcher who had been working with the PEBC project for the last three years, was seriously thinking about his future with Humaricare. He had just been offered a position with a medical research firm in St. Louis but was putting it off because he didn't know what was going to happen here. If he could be part of the research team that successfully developed the PEBC abortion pill, his future would be assured, no matter where he wound up.

Dr. Trailins walked by a computer station, then stopped and looked at it. This was the terminal that Dr. Louis King used to use. Dr. King was on a research trip to Sweden right now and had been gone for over a week. Dr. Trailins suddenly had an idea. Was it possible that Dr. King had taken his computer off-line before he left?

Trailins turned it on. After a few clicks and

beeps the screen came up. He typed in a file name he had been working with.

C:/WAVE.EXE.

The word "searching" came up, and Trailins caught his breath in excitement. That had not happened before. Before, every time he had tried to call up a file, any file, the "File not found" icon would come up immediately.

The screen turned blue, then his report appeared.

"Ah!" he shouted excitedly. "It's here! It's all here!" He picked up the telephone to call Dr. Corrigan. When Corrigan didn't answer, he called Dr. Kasabian.

"Dr. Kasabian," she answered.

"Dr. Kasabian, this is Victor Trailins. We haven't lost everything!" he said excitedly.

"What? What are you talking about?"

"I'm back in the lab at King's computer station. On a whim, I decided to call up my wave file, and, sure enough, there it was. It's still on the disk!"

"Well, I'm glad everything wasn't lost," Dr. Kasabian said.

"No, you don't understand! If *my* wave file is still there, so is everything else! I put that file on three weeks ago! Don't you see, Doctor? King must've taken his computer off-line before he left. It isn't connected with the others, therefore it wasn't affected by the virus."

"Wait a minute! You mean there's a chance that our entire files are—"

"Still on King's hard disk, yes. That's exactly what I mean," Trailins said excitedly.

"Listen, don't go away, don't touch anything, and don't tell anyone," Dr. Kasabian said. "I'm coming back there right now."

Trailins waited a few minutes, wanting to look through the files, but frightened to touch anything for fear he might lose it. Finally he saw Dr. Kasabian, walking swiftly, brushing her hair back from her forehead.

"Where is it?" she asked.

"Right here."

"And it isn't connected to the others?"

"No."

Dr. Kasabian sat down to the computer and made a few strokes. A new file came up.

"This is wonderful!" she said.

She called up another file, then another and another.

"Get me some disks," she said. "I'm going to back these up."

"Don't you think we ought to go ahead and load these files into the other computers?"

"Yes, but first I want to back them up."

"I'm going to have to get some more floppies. I know we don't have enough for all this."

"I only need one floppy."

"Dr. Kasabian, there's an awful lot of information on that hard disk. You're going to need twenty or thirty floppies at least."

"Not for the file I need," Dr. Kasabian said. "One will do."

Trailins walked over to a table and pulled open a drawer, then took out a 3.5 floppy disk. "Here," he said. "This one is all formatted and ready to go."

"As soon as I finish here, you get in touch with the others, then get all the information back on the hard disks. Then take one of them off-line. I don't want to take a chance on there being some residual virus."

"I bet Dr. Corrigan is going to be pleasantly surprised," Trailins suggested.

"He's going to be surprised," Dr. Kasabian replied.

Police Station

The uniformed officer escorted the woman into the bay area, then pointed toward the abutted desks of Briscoe and Logan.

"There they are, ma'am," he said. Then, louder, "Lennie, Mike, this lady is here to see you."

The two officers looked up from their desk. When Logan saw the beautiful woman standing there, he was the first to react.

"Mrs. Gray. Hello," he said, standing up quickly. He walked over to greet her. "Come over and sit down. Would you like a cup of coffee?"

"No, thank you," Mrs. Gray replied nervously. She looked around the bay. "I've never been in this part of a police station before."

"Nothing to it. It's just like a big office with a lot of desks," Logan explained. He escorted her over to his and Briscoe's part of the room.

Briscoe greeted her, then excused himself. A moment later he returned with Lieutenant Van Buren.

"Mrs. Gray, this is Lieutenant Van Buren, our boss," he said. "Lieutenant, this is Jerry Talbot's sister."

"How do you do," Van Buren said. "Gentlemen, where are your manners? Didn't you offer her any coffee?"

"I did, but she didn't want any."

"No, I, uh, won't be here long," Mrs. Gray said. "My business won't take much time."

"I see. And what business is that, Mrs. Gray? Why are you here?" Van Buren asked.

"It's about my brother. He isn't guilty, you know. He had nothing at all to do with the shooting."

"I'd like to believe that, Mrs. Gray, really I would," Logan said. "But he made things pretty difficult for himself when he took off running the way he did. If he is innocent, I'd like to hear it from his own lips."

"Yes, well, that's why I'm here. I'm going to arrange that," Mrs. Gray said nervously.

"You're going to tell us where to find him?" Briscoe asked.

"Not exactly."

"What do you mean, 'not exactly'?" Lieutenant Van Buren asked.

"Instead of telling you where to find him, I've decided to bring him in myself. He's here with me now."

"What?" Logan looked around. "Where?"

"He's waiting downstairs," Mrs. Gray explained. "My lawyer is with him."

"I'll go get him and bring him up to one of the interrogation rooms," Logan said.

"Use Room A," Lieutenant Van Buren suggested.

"All right," Briscoe said.

"May I be in there with you when you talk to him?" Mrs. Gray asked.

"No, I'm sorry, but only his lawyer can be with him," Lieutenant Van Buren explained.

"I understand," Mrs. Gray replied. "I . . . I hope I don't come to regret this. I'm very frightened about how this is all going to turn out. If I did the wrong thing . . ."

"You did the right thing, Mrs. Gray," Van Buren said. "Believe me, for all concerned, you did the right thing."

Chapter Four

Interrogation Room A

Talbot's lawyer was around seventy. He didn't look like the criminal lawyers Briscoe and Logan saw most frequently. He did wear an expensive toupee badly, which many criminal lawyers did, but he also had expensive clothes and a polished manner which was more in keeping with a corporate lawyer than one who dealt with the dregs of society. As it turned out, he was a corporate lawyer, responsible for handling the affairs of Pauline's.

"I am Crader Gilmore," the lawyer said, as he and Talbot took a seat across the table from Briscoe and Logan. "I informed Pauline and Jerry that this sort of thing is somewhat beyond my normal experience. They have agreed that if

I feel it is necessary, we will bring in another lawyer.''

"Do you want another lawyer during the questioning?'' Briscoe asked. "We'll be glad to wait.''

"No,'' Gilmore said. "I think I can get him through this part.''

"Mr. Talbot, I am going to read you your rights, although I'm sure Mr. Gilmore has already explained them to you.''

"Yes,'' Talbot said. "He has.''

Briscoe read him his rights, then asked if he understood.

"Yes, I understand. Ask your questions.''

"Where were you between six P.M. August eleventh, and seven A.M. August twelfth?''

"From about five-thirty until nine or so on the night of the eleventh, I was in the library. After that I walked around for a while, then I went back to my apartment. I read until about nine-thirty, then I went to bed.''

"Did anyone see you in the library?''

"Who knows?'' Talbot shrugged. "You've been to libraries, haven't you? Do you really notice who else is in there? You just sort of sit by yourself and get lost in a book or a magazine or something.''

"Did you eat dinner anywhere? Maybe go to a restaurant?''

"I stopped at a little deli and bought a sandwich."

"What time was that?"

"About five." Talbot brightened. "I've been there before. They know me . . . they'll vouch for me."

Briscoe shook his head. "It doesn't matter. Dr. Shaw was still alive at five."

"Oh."

"Did you visit the clinic on the eleventh?" Logan asked.

"Yes," Talbot started, but Crader Gilmore stuck out his hand and stopped him from going any further. "No," Talbot said, waving Gilmore's concern away. "I will not turn my back on what I have been doing, nor on the people who are involved in this crusade with me." Talbot looked back at Logan. "I was there at about four o'clock that afternoon, giving encouragement and moral support to the people who were manning the picket line."

"Did you come back later? Perhaps to carry your protest a little further?"

"I didn't kill Dr. Shaw."

"I didn't ask you that. I asked you if you came back later that evening."

"Why would I come back later?"

"You are avoiding the question, Mr. Talbot. Did you come back that night?"

"Jerry, you don't have to answer that question," Gilmore said.

"What makes you think I came back?" Talbot asked, waving his lawyer's protest aside.

"I think you came back to put up a poster," Logan said. "This poster in particular." He showed Talbot a photograph of the poster of the pregnant woman, holding the gun to her abdomen.

"My client has already told you he didn't come back," Gilmore said. "He has answered the question. Why do you continue to ask it?"

"He has not answered the question, Mr. Gilmore. He has avoided it. Were you there, Mr. Talbot?"

"I told you, I was there around four."

"This poster was not on the wall at four . . . nor even at five. But it *was* on the wall the next morning, which means someone put it up during the night. You have been arrested before, Mr. Talbot. We have your fingerprints on file. It was a very easy matter to compare the fingerprints on the poster with the prints on your file."

"And what did you find?" Talbot asked.

"We found that it was a perfect match," Briscoe said.

Gilmore was obviously shocked by the revelation, and he turned to look at Talbot in surprise.

"You came back during the night, didn't you, Talbot?" Logan asked.

Talbot's breathing grew more audible, and he brushed his hand through his hair.

"All right, yes, I came back," he said quietly.

"You put up the poster?"

"Yes, I'll admit I put up the poster. But I didn't kill Dr. Shaw."

"Who did?"

"I don't know who did."

"I think you do know, Mr. Talbot. Because if you didn't do it, then it had to be the person who was with you."

"The person with me?" Talbot asked, leaning forward with an expression of confusion on his face. "What are you talking about? There wasn't anyone with me."

"Come on, Talbot, you've been around. Are you planning on taking the fall by yourself?"

"I'm telling the truth. There was no one with me."

"We have proof there was someone with you," Logan said. "We have another set of fingerprints from the scene, and they aren't yours. They aren't the fingerprints of anyone who works there. That means there was someone with you that night. And you want to hear something interesting? Those same fingerprints are on the front of Shaw's desk, which puts that person in Shaw's office. Now, do you still want to say no one else was there?''

"Who was it, Talbot? Who are you trying to protect?" Briscoe asked.

"I'm not trying to protect anyone," Talbot insisted. "I don't know what you're talking about. I was there, yes. And I put the poster on the wall. But I was alone . . . absolutely alone."

"Come off that, Talbot. We're not playing games here. I told you—we have fingerprints!" Logan shouted, slapping the palm of his hand loudly on the table.

"Detective, what time were those fingerprints left?" Gilmore asked.

"What?"

"You have two sets of fingerprints, my client's, and this mysterious other person's fingerprints," Gilmore said. "But you have no way of knowing what time either of them were left, do you? My client could have been there before, after, or during the same time, and there would be no difference in the fingerprints. Is that right?"

Frustrated, Logan leaned back in his seat. "That's right," he grunted.

"Well, then, your prints don't prove anything except that someone else was there, and that someone is, in all probability, your most likely candidate for the murderer. After all, it was his

. . . or her fingerprints you found on Dr. Shaw's desk. Not Mr. Talbot's. Am I correct?''

"Yeah," Logan said. "You're correct."

"Then I suggest you leave my client alone, and go after the murderer."

"Talbot, what time did you come back to the clinic?" Briscoe asked, ignoring Gilmore's suggestion.

"Well, I—"

There was the sound of a chair scraping on the floor as Crader Gilmore pushed it back so he could get up. He put his hand out to stop Talbot from saying anymore.

"Jerry, I advise you now, don't go any further. Don't say one more word until we can get you another lawyer . . . one who is more competent in this sort of thing. I have to tell you, I would be doing you a disservice if I attempted to represent you any further."

"I don't need another lawyer, Mr. Gilmore," Talbot said. "I didn't kill Dr. Shaw, but to deny that I put up that poster, or to deny that I was there that night, would be to deny who I am and what I am all about. If there is any good to come out of all this, it will be to call attention to the abortion mills across the nation." He looked across the table at Logan and Briscoe and grinned broadly. "Look, I didn't kill Shaw. In fact, he was still alive when I left the clinic."

"Still alive? How do you know?"

"Because I saw him."

"Where?"

"In his office."

"Did you speak to him?"

"No. After I came in, I heard someone talking in the back. I sneaked down the hall to see who it was, and when I looked in through the crack of the door, I saw Dr. Shaw sitting at his desk, talking on the telephone."

"Who was he talking with?"

"I don't have any idea. All I know is I heard him say, 'You know damn well what's wrong. We need to talk and we need to talk now.' I didn't hear anything after that, because I left. Now, if you want to charge me with murder, you go right ahead and file your charges. Do your damnedest, officers. I welcome my trial. In fact, I'm looking forward to it."

"I'm warning you, Jerry. It will be quite dangerous to try and turn your trial into a show trial," Gilmore cautioned. "If you should lose, the consequences would be disastrous."

"Disastrous? No, the results of my trial, regardless of the outcome, will not be disastrous. Embarrassing perhaps. Maybe even discomfiting. But on the scale of things in the real world, it will not be disastrous. And if it draws attention to the wholesale slaughter of babies, then I will gladly become the sacrificial lamb, going to jail if need be," Jerry replied. "I'm ready for my trial. How soon can we start?"

"Before we get to the trial, we have a few more questions to ask."

"Ask them, I'll answer."

"Jerry, no! I must insist!" Gilmore said.

"Mr. Gilmore, I know that you have my best interests at heart," Talbot said. "But I am not afraid of the truth. I will answer the questions."

Gilmore put his head on his hands, causing his toupee to skew a little. He shook his head. "Very well, answer the questions. But I want you to remember that I don't approve of this, Jerry. I don't approve of this at all."

"You said you were there at four that afternoon," Logan said, continuing the questioning.

"That's right," Talbot replied. "I came to offer encouragement to the men and women who were working the picket line."

"Who was on the line at that time?"

"I'm not sure I know all of their names. I know some of them."

"Tell me the names you do know."

"Let me see . . . there was Father McKenna, of course. He was the team leader that day. And Alice Algood, Bert Carmody, Paul Alfusco, Jeanie Densberg. There may have been two or three more . . . I can't remember."

"But the names you just mentioned, the

priest, and the others, you're sure they were there?"

"Yes. Those, I'm sure of."

"Okay, so you went back, later, to put up the poster."

"Yes. Actually, I just sort of found myself down there. I didn't know I was going to put up a poster, but when I noticed that the door was unlocked, I just decided to take advantage of it."

"What time was that?"

"I don't know. Between ten-thirty and eleven that night, I guess."

"Were any of the demonstrators still there?"

"Oh, heavens no. They had all gone home long before that."

"What did you do?"

"Like I said, when I saw that the door was unlocked, I just opened it and walked in."

"Were you surprised by that?"

"Yes, very."

"Did anyone see you there?"

"I don't think so."

"Did you go into any of the other rooms?"

"Not at first. I went straight to the wall of the reception area and pinned up my poster. Then I heard someone on the telephone, so I sneaked down to see who was there. That was when I saw Dr. Shaw."

"When you were out front, putting up your

poster, did you notice anything out of the ordinary?" Briscoe asked.

"Like what?"

"Like the file cabinets being open? The papers strewn about the floor? The computers? The broken glass? You didn't notice any of that?"

"I didn't notice anything unusual about the file cabinets. There were no papers scattered about, and no broken glass on the floor. I didn't notice anything about the computer."

"You still insist that you were all alone?"

"Yes, I was all alone."

"Then do you have any idea who might have come in later to tear up the papers, scatter the files, break the front glass, disrupt the computers?" Briscoe asked.

"No, I don't know."

"Come now, Mr. Talbot. Surely you have an idea of who else in your organization might have such . . . zeal?" Logan said.

Talbot shook his head. "I have no idea who did it."

"But it had to be someone in your group, right?"

"I suppose so. Or, if not in my group, then someone who shares my vision."

"So sometime after you were there, this person who shares your . . . vision," Logan let the word "vision" slide out sarcastically, "whoever he or she is, came in and, perhaps figuring that the poster wasn't enough, emptied the file cabinets and deleted the computer files. Then, just for good measure, they knocked off Dr. Shaw."

Talbot stared across the table, his eyes unflinching. "You're the policeman, not I," he said. "If that's the theory you've come up with, it's as good as any. All I can tell you is, I did put up the poster. But I did not empty the file cabinets or mess with the computer. And I damn sure didn't kill Dr. Shaw. Also, there was no one with me. I was absolutely alone."

"Mr. Talbot, do you know the caliber of the bullet that killed Dr. Shaw?"

"No, should I?"

"It was a nine millimeter bullet, Mr. Talbot. Is that just an interesting coincidence?"

"Coincidence? Coincidence for what? I don't know what you're talking about. As a matter of fact, I don't know the caliber of any bullet, let alone that bullet. I've never really been interested in such things."

"Is that so, Mr. Talbot? Then how do you explain the box of nine millimeter shells that we found in your apartment?"

"Oh, is that what they were? Nine millimeter? I have no way of knowing," Talbot said calmly.

Logan drummed his fingers on the table in frustration. "Would you mind telling me what you're doing with a box of nine millimeter shells in your apartment, if you don't even know what they are?"

"My sister gave them to me a couple of years ago," Talbot answered.

"Your sister? You mean Mrs. Gray? Why would she give you bullets?" Briscoe asked.

Talbot laughed. "It wasn't exactly a birthday present. Jason Gray, her husband, was going through the last stages of lung cancer. She was afraid he might shoot himself, so she brought me his gun and bullets. After he died, she took the gun back, but she forgot the bullets and I never got around to returning them."

"I can vouch for that, Sergeant," Gilmore said, coming up from his long, self-imposed silence. "Pauline was terribly afraid that Jason would take his own life."

"Do you have any more questions, officer?" Talbot asked.

Briscoe and Logan looked at each other, as if each were waiting for the other to ask the question that would put an end to the sparring. Neither could come up with such a question so, finally, Briscoe said, with a sigh, "No, that's all for now."

Talbot smiled. "Well, now that we have all that straight, when do we go to trial?"

* * *

Assistant D.A. Ben Stone looked up from his desk when he heard a knock on his door. He smiled.

"Hello Mike, Lennie," he said. "Come on in. Coffee?"

"No, thanks," Logan said. "I've been drinking it all day down at the station."

"I'll have some," Lennie put in. He smiled at Logan. "I'm surprised at you, Mike. Haven't you learned by now that the coffee you get here is much better than the mud we get down at the station house?"

"Don't be ridiculous, Lennie," Stone joked. "It's the same coffee. You just get our leftover the next day, that's all. What's on your mind?"

"We've picked up Jerry Talbot," Logan said.

"Where did you find him?"

"He came in. Rather, his sister and his lawyer brought him in."

"He surrendered to you?"

"Yes."

"Well, that's nice. Nothing like having our cases hand delivered, all done up in a neat little package."

"It's not quite that way," Briscoe said, returning with his cup. He blew on it before he took the first sip.

"What do you mean?"

"He hasn't confessed. He just surrendered."

"Wait a minute. Before we go any further, let

me get Claire in here. She seems to have taken a particular interest in this case." Stone picked up the phone and punched two numbers. A moment later he spoke into the receiver. "Claire? You want to come in here for a moment? Lennie and Mike are here. They've got Talbot."

Claire Kincaid arrived less than a minute later, a bundle of energy, carrying a yellow pad and a pencil.

"All right, good going, guys," she said enthusiastically. "Where did you find him?"

"You don't want to know," Logan said.

"Was it rough?"

"Rough? I'll say it was rough. Sometimes law enforcement can be a tough and dangerous business, but someone has to do it."

"Oh, my," Claire said. "And here I was being so flippant about it. I didn't even stop to think you might be risking your lives bringing him in. That was terribly insensitive of me. I'm sorry."

"The only thing Mike risked was nausea from looking at Crader Gilmore's bad toupee," Briscoe said with an irreverent chuckle.

Stone and Logan laughed.

"I beg your pardon?" Claire asked.

"Crader Gilmore is Talbot's lawyer. He brought Talbot in," Stone explained.

"Crader Gilmore is Talbot's lawyer?" Claire asked in surprise.

"Yes."

"I don't get it. What would he be doing defending Jerry Talbot? He's not a criminal lawyer. He's a corporate lawyer. I remember attending one of his lectures when I was in school."

"Crader Gilmore is Talbot's sister's lawyer. She's Pauline Gray," Logan said.

"Pauline Gray? I've heard that name somewhere," Stone said.

"Pauline's beauty salons," Claire asked. "There are about a dozen of them in New York. And you say she's Talbot's sister?"

"Yes," Logan answered.

"That's hard to believe. She's a very 'with-it' woman. I've read about her in newspapers and magazines. I would have a difficult time putting her with Jerry Talbot."

"I know what you mean," Logan said. "She's a beautiful, classy lady. He's pretty much a kook."

"You were saying, just before I called Claire, that Talbot had surrendered, but he hadn't confessed," Stone said.

"He has confessed to putting the poster up on the wall. He says he didn't do any of the other stuff, and he insists that Dr. Shaw was alive when he left."

"He talked to him?"

"He says he overheard him on the telephone.

He sneaked down the hall to have a look. Shaw was at his desk in his office."

"What time was that?"

"Ten-thirty or eleven," Briscoe answered.

"If we can put Talbot there at that time, then that has to make him the number-one suspect," Claire said.

"Yeah, well, he is aching for a trial."

"Good. If he wants a trial, let's give him one," Claire suggested.

"You don't understand, Miss Kincaid," Logan said. "He wants a show trial. He wants to get up on the witness stand and spout off his ideas. And he wants to do it alone. He says he knows nothing about the second intruder—the one whose fingerprints are on the files, and on the front of Shaw's desk."

"Maybe the prospect of a murder trial will cause him to have second thoughts about going it alone," Claire suggested. "Let's indict him, Ben."

Stone shook his head. "I don't know," he said. He looked at Briscoe and Logan. "I want you two to use your policeman's gut instinct here. What do you think about Talbot? Did he kill Shaw?"

"Ben, what are you doing?" Claire asked. "We can't select the cases we try on someone's 'gut instinct.' We need to use the rules of evidence to make up our minds."

"All right, what evidence do we have pointing to Jerry Talbot?" Stone asked.

"We have Talbot's confession that he put the poster up," Briscoe said. "And we have his fingerprints on that poster. We also have a box of nine millimeter shells which were taken from his apartment."

"No ballistics match?"

"No ballistics, no gun," Briscoe said. "Talbot claims that the bullets we found in his apartment came from his sister when she feared that her husband might be suicidal during a terminal illness. Gilmore backs him up in that claim, and so does his sister. I'm afraid it would be hard to crack that story."

"Yes, but don't forget we have the letters T-A that Shaw scratched on a tablet, just before he died," Logan said. "That could have been the first two letters of Talbot's name."

Stone sighed and shook his head. "All that gives us is a string of circumstantial evidence, not strong enough by itself, nor in concert, to get a conviction," he said.

"It's enough to convince the grand jury," Claire insisted. "You know it is. And if we can just get the case to trial, a really strong presentation could win it. We can make the case, Ben. I know we can."

Stone looked at Briscoe and Logan. "I'll ask

my question again. What are your instincts about this? Is Talbot guilty?"

Briscoe and Logan looked at each other for a moment, then Briscoe sighed.

"Mike and I have talked about it, Ben," he said. "The truth is, neither one of us think Talbot is guilty. He wants whatever publicity he can get from the trial. But we don't think he killed the doc."

"Then who did?" Claire asked.

"We think it was whoever the other person was. Whether he was with Talbot, or whether he came in later," Briscoe said.

"Do you have any idea who that might be?" Ben asked.

"Not the slightest idea."

"Wait a minute! What about the note?" Claire asked. "T-A for Talbot. Shaw was clearly trying to tell us who killed him."

"If he wrote the note," Briscoe said.

"What do you mean? Of course he wrote it."

"He was shot in the heart," Briscoe explained. "Death was instantaneous. I don't see how he had time to write anything."

"Maybe he started the note and was shot in the middle of writing it."

"If that's the case, why didn't Talbot—if Talbot is the one—take the note with him?"

"Have you given the note to someone for

handwriting analysis to see if it was Shaw's handwriting?" Stone asked.

"No."

"It wouldn't hurt to get it analyzed," Stone said. "But even if we do get it analyzed and it turns out to be Shaw's handwriting, I still don't think we could sustain a murder charge."

"That's it, then? We're just going to let Talbot walk?" Claire asked in exasperation.

"What else can we do?" Stone asked.

"Damnit, Ben, I can't believe this."

"Claire, think about it. If we indict before we have enough material to guarantee a conviction, we're playing right into Talbot's hands. He'll have the entire country to preach to." Stone looked up at Logan and Briscoe. "Sorry, guys. It looks like you're going to have to start all over again."

"That's okay, I've got an idea where we could start," Briscoe suggested.

"I'm glad you have an idea, because I'm fresh out," Stone said.

"How about Father McKenna?" Briscoe asked. "Didn't Talbot say he was the team leader for the group that was there the day before?"

Chapter Five

Father McKenna stood when Briscoe and Logan were shown into his office.

"Good afternoon, gentlemen," he said. "I wondered when you would get around to talking to me. Please, please, have a seat."

"You mean you've been expecting this?" Briscoe asked as the two sat in chairs the priest made ready for them. He moved back to his own seat behind his desk.

"Oh, yes, yes," he said, smiling broadly. "I'm a great mystery fan, you see. I read all the books and watch all the shows on television. I figured you'd have to touch all the bases, and I knew I was one of those bases. I know that you are looking for Jerry Talbot, so let me hasten to say that

I don't have the slightest idea where he might be."

"We have him," Briscoe said.

"You found him?"

"Actually, Father, he gave himself up," Logan said.

"He did? Well then, good for him. I'm sure it will be much better this way. I am curious, though. What does he say about this?"

"He says he didn't kill the doctor."

"Yes, I'm quite sure he didn't."

"Why are you so sure?"

"I have no proof, if that's what you mean. It's just my belief in Jerry."

"Being as how you're a mystery fan, Father, have you done any amateur sleuthing?" Briscoe asked. "Do you have any ideas about who might have killed Dr. Shaw?"

"No. I have thought about it, but I don't have a clue. I must admit that it has me perplexed."

"What if I told you that Talbot confessed to having been down there that night? Could you believe that?"

"Jerry told you that he was at the clinic? Why was he there, did he say?"

"He says he came to put up the poster."

"Oh, that dreadful poster. You mean the one with the pregnant young woman holding a gun to her distended abdomen. I don't like it, you know. I've told Jerry that I believe it alienates more people than it could possibly attract to our cause."

"Do you have any problem in believing that Talbot put up the poster?"

"No. Jerry is very active and very passionate in his stand on abortion. I can believe that he broke in, scattered the files, and put up the poster. But I still don't believe he had anything to do with Dr. Shaw's death."

"Actually, he doesn't even admit to breaking in and scattering the files. He claims that he walked in through an unlocked door and did nothing but put the poster on the wall."

"That's odd. Who do you suppose did the other?"

"That's what we were hoping you could tell us," Briscoe said.

Father McKenna shook his head. "I'm sorry. I don't know."

"Talbot said you were the team leader for your group."

"Yes, Wednesday's Children."

"I beg your pardon?"

"Wednesday's Children. That's what we call our team. We report for duty every Wednesday, you see."

"Would you mind telling me who's on your team? And also, if you would, tell me a little about each of them."

"All right, I can't see any harm in that. Let's

see, there's Bert Carmody. He's a very good man, a member of my church in fact. He's an insurance salesman, he's married and has three kids. Then there's Jeanie Densberg, she's a college student who has been very active. And Alice Algood and her sister, Marcie Terrell. Alice is a housewife, Marcie works in a day care center. There's also Bill Patterson. I don't know too much about him, he just joined us recently. And of course there's Paul Alfusco. He's rather quiet, though he feels things very deeply. The 'still waters run deep' thing, I suppose."

"Alfusco?" Briscoe asked.

"Yes. He's a free-lance journalist, I believe."

"And he's on your team? On Wednesday?"

"Yes. Why are you particularly interested in him?"

"We met him the next morning. Is it common for your people to be on more than one day?"

"Not really," Father McKenna answered. "We try to discourage that, actually. You see, sometimes there are occasions of civil disobedience resulting in arrests. By having separate teams like this, we feel we can minimize any damage which might be done to the organization by a wholesale arrest." Father McKenna chuckled. "It's rather like having watertight doors on board a ship, I imagine."

"Has Alfusco ever been arrested for civil disobedience?" Logan asked.

"Are you serious? You don't remember Paulie Alfusco?"

Logan shook his head.

"Damn it," Briscoe said, snapping his fingers. "I knew there was something familiar about him. He's that Alfusco?"

"One and the same. He hasn't lost a bit of his passion, despite aging a few years. Only now, instead of protesting the war, he's protesting abortion."

"Who is this guy, Paulie Alfusco?" Logan asked.

"I can't believe you've never heard of him," Briscoe replied. "They used to mention his name in the same breath as Dr. Spock, Jane Fonda, Father Berrigan. He burned draft cards, established an underground railroad to smuggle draft dodgers out of the country. He was a real thorn."

"That which you consider a thorn was considered a hero by others," Father McKenna said. "For those of us who opposed the war, Paulie Alfusco was an inspiration. He wrote a book about all that, you know. It was called *Bombs and Barricades*. Have you ever read it?"

"No."

"Apparently, not many people did," Father McKenna explained. "After the excitement of the war protest ended and his book fizzled, he sort of dropped out of the limelight. He's made a living ever since then writing articles and short stories for magazines and newspapers. I thought his days of activism were over. Then he showed up a couple of weeks ago and offered to help us protest what was going on at Humaricare. I felt very honored."

"Father McKenna, do you know where Alfusco lives?" Briscoe asked.

"No, I'm sorry. I'm afraid I don't."

"How do you get hold of him?" Logan asked.

"I don't get hold of him. He just shows up."

Briscoe stood and stuck his hand out. "Thank you, Father. You have been most helpful."

"I hope I have been," Father McKenna said. "I believe the earlier you solve this crime, the better it will be for all of us. I consider abortion a terrible thing, and I will protest against it as spiritedly as I know how. But no matter how passionate my feelings are against what they are attempting to do in that clinic, it does not justify taking a man's life. And I don't think Jerry Talbot, or Paulie Alfusco, or anyone else connected with Action Committee for Life Watch, had anything to do with the murder."

Police station

"Here's Paul Alfusco's file," Briscoe said, dropping a folder on the desk in front of Logan.

Logan opened it, then laughed.

"What is it?"

"Look at this picture," he said. "Long hair, beard, beads, paisley shirt. Isn't that something?"

"What did you look like then?" Briscoe asked.

Logan laughed again. "Now that you mention it, I guess I looked pretty much like that. But I was just a kid. It was a fashion thing for me, not a social statement. How about you?"

"Short hair, clean-shaven, I always was pretty much of a straight-arrow."

"Yeah, I guess I could believe that," Logan said. He studied the photo on the file before him. "He sure doesn't look like this picture today," Logan said. "I mean when we were talking to him the other day, he looked pretty much like a middle-aged accountant."

"Yeah, well, here's something that won't change," Briscoe said, pulling out the fingerprint card. He took it over to one of the computers and scanned it onto the screen, then brought it across one of the prints they had lifted from the desk in Shaw's office.

"Well, now, isn't technology wonderful?" he said a moment later. He leaned back in his chair. "Take a look, Mike," he invited.

Logan looked at the screen and saw that the two fingerprints were a perfect match.

"Let's go pick him up."

"Where? The address in his record file is twenty-five years old."

"Maybe he's still there."

"Not unless he lives in a parking garage," Briscoe said. "I know that address. Hand me the telephone book."

Paul Alfusco wasn't listed in the telephone book, and the address the city collector had for him was a dead end. They were equally unsuccessful in getting an address from the rest of "Wednesday's Children." Like Father McKenna, they said that he just showed up on the days they were to make their protest.

"This is ridiculous," Briscoe told Lieutenant Van Buren. "I mean it's not like this guy is on the run or anything. As far as I know, he doesn't even know we're looking for him. He isn't hiding, but I can't find him."

"He has to work somewhere, doesn't he?" Van Buren asked.

"He works for himself. He's a free-lance writer," Logan explained.

"Wait a minute, what was the name of that book?" Briscoe said. "The one Father McKenna said he wrote?"

"Bombs and Barricades."

"Maybe we could find out who published it. They might know how to get hold of him," Briscoe suggested.

"Just a minute," Van Buren said. She began writing on a little piece of paper. "Here." She handed the paper to Logan.

"What is this?"

"It's the address of a used and rare bookstore. The woman who owns it is Miss Jane Templeton. We go back a long way together. Have a visit with her. She may not have that book, but I guarantee you she'll have the title listed somewhere. And if she has the title, she'll have the publishing information."

Briscoe smiled. "Do you feel literary?" he asked Logan.

"Lead on, McDonald," Logan said.

Van Buren laughed. "You going out for a hamburger? That's 'lead on McDuff.' "

"Whatever."

The bookstore was on Seventy-third Street. It was long, narrow, dark, and high. Ladders on tracks reached up to the top of towering book stacks. Tables, piled high with books, were surrounded by browsers. There was a moldy, musty smell to the place, as if the air had been imported direct from the eighteenth century. Brisco figured that was quite possible, since a prominent sign advertised this as the "largest stock of eighteenth century books in New York."

A young girl with straight brown hair and large, oval, wire-rim glasses was behind the cash register.

"May I help you?" she asked.

"We're with the police," Logan said. "Would Jane Templeton be in?"

"She's upstairs," the young girl said. She pointed to the back of one of the stacks and a narrow, winding stairway. "Just go up those stairs. She has a desk in the back. You can't miss her."

"Thanks."

Jane Templeton was about sixty, with gray hair pulled back in a bun and pierced with a pencil. She was wearing a broach watch, pinned to her blouse. She looked nothing at all like Briscoe thought she would. He smiled at how wrong he was, and she looked up just in time to catch it.

"Are you amused?" she asked.

"What? Oh, no, I'm sorry," Briscoe replied, caught off guard by her challenge. He pointed to the watch. "It's just that I haven't seen a watch like that since I was in grade school. One of my teachers wore one."

Miss Templeton chuckled. "That's where I got this one," she said. "From a lady who taught in the school where I used to be the librarian. Now, can I help you?"

"I hope so," Briscoe said. "We're police officers."

The woman smiled. "Really? One of my favorite people is a police officer. She used to just live in my library. Her name is Anita Van Buren; though, as big as the department is, I'm sure there's not much chance you would know her."

"On the contrary. We do know her. That's why we're here. She thought you might be able to help us," Briscoe said. "We're looking for a book that's out of print for a long time."

"I have books in here that were published before this nation became a country. How long has the book you've been looking for been out of print?"

Brisco laughed. "Not that long, I'm sure."

"It's *Bombs and Barricades*," Logan said. "By Paul Alfusco."

"What a perfectly awful book," she said. "Why in heaven's name would you want to read it?"

"What? You mean you *know* the book?"

"Yes, I know it." She got up from her desk and walked over to one of the shelves. "I even have a few of them. Every now and then I'll get someone in who is a student of the sixties, and they have a prescribed list of books they're trying to round up. *Bombs and Barricades* is a curiosity from that era, and I do believe it has sold more as a curiosity than it ever did while it was still on the shelves. Ah, yes, here it is."

"Who published it?"

"Crestwood House."

"Crestwood House? Where is that?"

Miss Templeton laughed. "Oh, heavens, Crestwood House is no longer in business. I'm afraid it has gone the way of so many fine, old publishing houses. It's either been gobbled up or is out of business entirely."

"Well, so much for that idea," Logan said disgustedly.

"What are you trying to do?"

"We're trying to find out where Alfusco lives," Briscoe explained. "I thought maybe his publisher might know."

"Why don't you try *Timewarp*?"

"*Timewarp*?"

"It's a science fiction magazine. Alfusco had a story in it last month."

Briscoe smiled broadly. "Thank you, Miss Templeton, you've been a big help."

"Tell Anita I send her a great big hello, would you?"

"You've got it," Briscoe called back over his shoulder.

Timewarp magazine advertised itself with a little brass plaque on the wall just inside the door of a building in the 200 block of Fifth Avenue. The directory inside led them to the seventh floor, where they saw the name again on the frosted glass of a door. There was no desk inside, just a sofa, chair, and table. The table was piled high with what appeared to be manuscripts.

"Is that you, Drake?" a man called from another room.

"No, we're police officers," Briscoe called back.

"Police officers?" A smallish, gray-haired man with a white shirt and bow tie appeared in the door. He was wearing sleeve garters and holding a batch of papers in one hand and a blue pen in the other. "Is something wrong? Has something happened to Drake?" he asked anxiously.

"No, we're just looking for some information, that's all. I'm Sergeant Briscoe, this is Detective Logan."

"I'm Carson Jefferies, the publisher and owner of *Timewarp*. What can I do for you?"

"Mr. Jefferies, we're trying to locate one of your writers," Briscoe said.

At that moment the door behind them

opened and a plump, dark-haired woman appeared. Jefferies smiled in relief.

"Gentlemen, this is my daughter, Drake. We are a two-man operation here . . . or, rather a one-man and one-woman operation. I handle the editorial and Drake handles everything else. I'm sure she can be of much more help to you than I could, and I simply must get this finished today. Drake, these men are policemen."

"What can I do for you?" Drake asked.

"We're trying to find one of your writers . . . a man named Paul Alfusco," Briscoe said. "I understand he did a story for you last month."

"It ran last month," Drake said. "We bought it last year."

"Do you, by any chance, have his address?"

"Just a minute." Drake opened a large ledger book, and Logan chuckled. She looked up in question.

"I'm sorry," Logan said. "It's just that this is a science fiction magazine. You publish things about rocket ships and robots and such, but you use an old-fashioned ledger book instead of a computer."

"I am more comfortable with a ledger book," Drake explained without apology. She began running her finger down the columns. "Ah, here it is. We don't have an address for him, other than a post office box number. Ooops, sorry, we don't even have that. The last thing we sent to that address was returned, with no forwarding address."

"God, I hope this guy never decides to go into hiding," Logan said. "The sunlight wouldn't even be able to find him."

"You might try his bank," Drake said simply.

"I beg your pardon?"

"He's written five stories for us over the last three years. All of the checks we sent him were cashed at the same bank, same branch."

"Madam, you are a genius!" Briscoe said.

"Yes, I know," Drake replied matter-of-factly. "It can be a burden sometimes."

Armed with a warrant, Briscoe and Logan checked the bank's files and found a mailing address for the statements. When they knocked on the door of Alfusco's apartment a half hour later, he answered the door.

"Mr. Alfusco?" Briscoe said.

Alfusco held up a finger.

"I suppose you want me to go down to the station with you?" he said. "Let me turn off the coffeepot and I'll be right with you."

"We'll come with you," Briscoe said.

"No need. I'll be right . . ." Alfusco paused in mid-sentence, then smiled. "You're afraid I'll run, aren't you?"

"That thought did cross my mind," Briscoe said.

"Not to worry, Sergeant. It is Sergeant, isn't it?"

"Yes."

"I have no intention of running, Sergeant. I am too old and too out of shape for anything like that."

"Humor me," Briscoe said. "We're coming with you."

Police station, one hour later

"Where is he?" Stone asked.

"We've got him back in Interrogation Room A," Briscoe answered.

"Have you talked to him yet?"

"No, we thought it might be better if you did. We do have something for you, though."

"What's that?"

"We searched his apartment and turned up an empty shell casing. A nine millimeter."

"What does the lab say? Will they be able to tell if it matches up with the bullet they took out of Shaw?"

"Within a five percent margin of error. They're running the comparison now."

"Good. Now, let's go speak with Mr. Alfusco."

Logan was standing just outside the interrogation room drinking a cup of coffee and looking through the one-way mirror at Alfusco. Alfusco was sitting, with his hands folded on the table in front of him.

"How's our man doing?" Briscoe asked.

"He's been pretty calm so far," Logan said. "He's looked at his watch several times."

"Let's see what he has to say," Stone suggested. He opened the door to go in, and Briscoe and Logan went with him.

"Mr. Alfusco, my name is Benjamin Stone. I am the Assistant District Attorney."

"I've been in here quite a while, Mr. Stone," Alfusco replied. "I'm working on a story and I have a deadline. I'd like to get back to it."

"I'm sure you would, Mr. Alfusco. But first I would like to ask you a few questions. Do you have a lawyer?"

"No," Alfusco answered.

"May I strongly recommend that you get one?"

Alfusco shook his head. "I don't need one."

"I'm afraid that you do, sir. You are being investigated for a murder."

"I assumed as much," Alfusco said.

Stone sighed and sat down. "All right, Mr. Alfusco. Let's get into the questioning. You are aware of your rights?"

"They were read to me," Alfusco said.

"Do you understand them?"

"Oh, yes, I understand them perfectly."

"Very well then, Mr. Alfusco, let's get started, shall we? Where were you on the night of the eleventh?"

"I respectfully decline to answer that question under the protection afforded me by the Fifth Amendment to the Constitution of the United States of America," Alfusco said.

"You refuse to answer the question?"

"That is my right, is it not?"

"Yes," Stone agreed. "Okay, then let's try this one. You were on the scene on the morning of the twelfth, were you not?"

"For the same reason as before, I refuse to answer your question."

"Mr. Alfusco, that is not an incriminating question. We know you were there. Sergeant Briscoe and Detective Logan both spoke with you."

Alfusco was silent.

"Are you a member of the group known as the Action Committee for Life Watch?"

"I respectfully decline to answer that question."

"Would it be asking too much to have you tell us whether you are pro-abortion or anti-abortion?"

Again Alfusco was silent.

"Then here is a question I would think you

will want to answer. Mr. Alfusco, did you kill Dr. Shaw?"

"I respectfully decline to answer that question," Alfusco said.

"Mr. Alfusco," Stone started, but the door to the interrogation room opened and Lieutenant Van Buren came in, carrying a paper. She handed it to Briscoe, who looked at it, smiled, then looked up.

"It's from the lab," he said. "Alfusco, the empty shell casing we found in your apartment matches up with the bullet that killed Dr. Shaw."

"We've got your fingerprints on Shaw's desk, we've got witnesses who can put you on the scene the day before and the day after the murder took place. And we have the shell casing from the fatal bullet, taken from your apartment," Logan said.

Stone looked at Alfusco, but Alfusco showed no reaction to the news.

"Mr. Alfusco, this is a very serious matter, sir. I strongly recommend that you get a lawyer and begin planning your defense."

Alfusco smiled broadly. "I don't need a lawyer, Mr. Stone. My defense has been planned and provided by the framers of the Constitution. I don't need to answer any questions . . . and I don't need to testify. Go ahead and make your case if you can. You'll make it without me."

Stone stood up and looked at Alfusco for a long moment. "Mr. Alfusco, I get the feeling that, somehow, you are playing a game. If you are, you are making a big mistake. Murder is not a game." He looked over at Briscoe. "Book him."

LAW &
ORDER

Chapter Six

"**S**ergeant Briscoe, Detective Logan, thank you for stopping by to see me," Father McKenna said. "Please, come into my office. Have a seat."

"You said you had something for us, Father?" Briscoe said as he sat in the proffered chair.

"Yes," Father McKenna said. "Well, in a matter of speaking, I do. I just wanted to tell you that you are barking up the wrong tree."

"What do you mean?" Logan asked.

"Paulie Alfusco," Father McKenna said. "He didn't kill Dr. Shaw."

"How do you know he didn't?"

"He told me he didn't."

Briscoe laughed. "Excuse me, Father, but that hardly seems like an exoneration."

"Has he told you?" Father McKenna asked.

"Told me what?"

"Has he told you that he was innocent?"

"No, he hasn't."

"In fact, he hasn't told you anything, has he? He is clinging to the Fifth Amendment, I believe."

"You've got that right," Briscoe said. "Father, if you have any influence over him, you might tell him that little ploy isn't going to work. He has the right not to incriminate himself, that's true. But he also has the right to deny the charges. The fact that he is refusing to speak on any issue at all is just making it more difficult for him."

"Yes, well, he did speak to me."

"Can you tell us?" Logan asked. "I mean, isn't what he says to a priest confidential?"

Father McKenna laughed. "He didn't make confession to me. Actually, he isn't even Catholic. No, I'm under no obligation to keep secret the gist of our conversation. On the contrary, I think that, under the circumstances, I am morally bound to share his conversation with you."

"All right, what did he tell you?"

"He told me he didn't do it."

"Did he explain how his fingerprints got all over the place? Did he tell you how the murder weapon turned up in his apartment?" Briscoe asked.

"He says he picked it up off Dr. Shaw's desk," Father McKenna said.

"You mean he admits he was there?" Logan asked.

"Yes."

"Not much of an admission, really," Briscoe said. "We had his fingerprints all over the place. But if what he's telling is true, why did he pick up the gun? Why didn't he leave it there?"

"I asked him the same thing," Father McKenna said.

"Did he answer you?"

Father McKenna shook his head. "No. All he said was that he picked up the gun because he thought it was the right thing to do."

"The right thing to do?" Logan shook his head in confusion. "You know what I think? I think he's laying in the groundwork for pleading not guilty by insanity. That's the craziest thing I've ever heard."

"Father McKenna," Briscoe said, "if you have any influence on him at all, you'll convince him to get a lawyer and give up this idiotic form of defense."

"I am trying," Father McKenna said.

When Briscoe and Logan returned to the station, they found Dr. Linda Kasabian waiting for them. She was butting out one cigarette and lighting another when Briscoe and Logan greeted her.

"I know," she said, answering the unasked question. "I'm a doctor. What am I doing smoking? I know all the intellectual reasons why I should not. But I haven't been able to find the willpower I need to stop."

"I've been around too long to judge," Briscoe said. He and Logan sat down. "So, what can we do for you, Doctor? Are you here to check on our progress?"

"Not exactly," Dr. Kasabian said. She took a long, audible puff. "There is something that has been bothering me since this all began. I should've said something about it at the time, but I felt like it would be an act of disloyalty to do so."

"Disloyalty? Disloyalty to who?" Briscoe asked.

"Disloyalty to Humaricare . . . to the PEBC project. Most of all, I guess, disloyalty to Dr. Corrigan."

"What are you trying to tell us, Doctor?" Logan asked.

"The information Dr. Corrigan gave you is incorrect."

Briscoe leaned forward. "What information?"

"The information about PEBC. We aren't exactly on the verge of a breakthrough. We aren't nearly as close to developing it as Dr. Corrigan wants everyone to believe.''

"That's it? That's what you've been agonizing over? Whether or not Dr. Corrigan told the truth about how close you were to developing that abortion pill?'' Logan said. "Dr. Kasabian, I admire your concern for the truth, but whether or not you're close to developing the pill has no bearing on our case. You shouldn't have been all that upset about it.''

"No, wait a minute,'' Briscoe said, sticking his hand out. He studied Dr. Kasabian's face for a long moment. "You believe there might be some connection, don't you?''

Biting her lower lip, Dr. Kasabian answered with a short nod of her head.

"Why do you think Dr. Corrigan would tell us that you were close, if you aren't?'' Briscoe asked.

"Money,'' she said simply. "A great deal of money. His decision to lie was a business decision, pure and simple, made to keep the shareholders happy.''

"Shareholders? Wait a minute. You mean Humaricare is a 'for profit' organization?'' Logan asked.

"Of course it is. What did you think it was?''

"I don't know. I guess I thought it was some foundation-funded research think tank.''

Dr. Kasabian laughed, a short, brittle laugh.

"How naive can you be? Detective Logan, you don't think for one moment that Humaricare's medical research is driven by some deep-rooted need to serve humanity, do you? I hate to disabuse you of that noble idea, but if we're successful, Humaricare will earn billions of dollars. That's billions, with a B. And, as long as those shareholders think we're on the verge of success, they'll keep the funding going."

"I'm going to ask the question that will move us from the naive to the cynic," Briscoe said. "Could it be that Dr. Corrigan might not really care whether you're successful or not?"

"Now you're beginning to understand," Dr. Kasabian said as she ground out her cigarette. "Of course it would be good if we were successful, but in Dr. Corrigan's case it is not an all or nothing deal. The PEBC project is budgeted at five million dollars per year. Dr. Corrigan is the administrator of that budget. It would be very much to his advantage to hold out the promise of imminent success, whether that promise is spurious or valid."

"I can see why he would want to mislead the shareholders, but how was he able to?" Briscoe asked. "Wouldn't he have had to back up his report with some documentation?"

"Dr. Corrigan had documentation, but it was based upon a faulty lab analysis. When Gary . . . that is, Dr. Shaw, read the report, he realized that the lab analysis was wrong and that Dr. Corrigan had purposely used faulty data to make his report to the shareholders look better.''

"What sort of faulty data?''

"Some information from a lab experiment was incorrectly recorded. The result made it look as if it had been a one-hundred-percent success, when in fact it was just the opposite. The mistake was found almost immediately and corrected, but when Dr. Corrigan made his report, he purposely used that faulty data to give results that were misleading.''

"And Dr. Shaw didn't agree with what Dr. Corrigan was doing?'' Logan asked, beginning to see the picture.

Dr. Kasabian shook her head. "No, not at all,'' she said. "In fact, they argued quite bitterly about it. Dr. Shaw said we had a moral and professional obligation to the truth. Dr. Corrigan took the position that, as Chief of Research, his principal responsibility was to see to the successful development of the pill, which meant ensuring the continuation of research money. Dr. Shaw replied that David had no principles . . . period.''

"Tell me, Dr. Kasabian, where did you fit into all this? Were you in support of Dr. Corrigan, or Dr. Shaw?''

"I was in support of the project and the

Humaricare clinic," Dr. Kasabian said. "And I was against anything that might separate these two, equally brilliant men. I tried to be the peacemaker. Unfortunately, I was unable to get them to resolve their differences. There was a bitter argument, and Dr. Shaw told Dr. Corrigan that if Dr. Corrigan didn't correct the report immediately, then he would. David told Gary not to do anything he would be sorry for. Gary asked him if he was threatening him, and David answered, coldly, that it was more of a promise than a threat. I grew frightened then, and I left."

"When was that?"

"That was Wednesday afternoon at about five or five-thirty. Nearly everyone else had left by then."

"Wednesday? That would be the eleventh?"

"Yes. As it turned out, that was the last time I saw Dr. Shaw alive."

"Are you suggesting that Dr. Corrigan carried out his threat?"

"No, not exactly. In fact, though I didn't see Dr. Shaw again, I did talk to him later that night. He called me from the office. He was still terribly upset, and he accused David of threatening him."

"Dr. Kasabian, let's not dance around the hat here," Logan said. "Are you here to suggest that Dr. Corrigan might have killed Dr. Shaw?"

"I . . . I'm not quite ready to make that suggestion," Dr. Kasabian said. "But I have been thinking about the possibility ever since that awful morning, especially given the heat of their argument the afternoon before. So I finally decided that I have no choice, I must tell you the truth about what happened regardless of the consequences. You're the expert in these matters. I leave it up to you to make a determination as to what it all means."

"Dr. Kasabian, were any others, besides you, Dr. Shaw, and Dr. Corrigan, present during their argument?" Briscoe asked.

"No. As I said, it was already past normal business hours."

"Was anyone else aware of the disagreement between the two men over this faulty laboratory analysis?"

"I don't know."

Briscoe ran his hand through his hair, then leaned back in his chair.

"You do see our dilemma now, don't you, Dr. Kasabian? If we confront Dr. Corrigan with the charge that he may have had a disagreement with Dr. Shaw over some falsified reports, all he would have to do is ask us to prove that the reports were falsified. And, without the file, we can't do that."

"Oh, but we do have the files," Dr. Kasabian said.

Briscoe and Logan looked at her in surprise.

"What? What are you talking about? I thought the virus wiped everything out."

"Computer viruses only work when computers are networked."

"Yes, but all the computers were networked, weren't they?"

"Normally that would be true. But there was one computer in the lab that wasn't connected to the others. One of our lab technicians, Dr. Victor Trailins, discovered it. It was a station normally used by another researcher, Louis King. But Dr. King left for Europe that very day. Evidently he took his computer off-line before he left, and as a result it wasn't affected by the virus. We've been able to totally reconstruct our files from the data that was on the hard disk of his computer."

"Do these files include that faulty lab report you were talking about?"

"Yes. And it also includes this."

Dr. Kasabian opened her purse and took out a 3.5-inch floppy disk, then handed it to Briscoe.

"What is this?"

"This is the Tairge file," Dr. Kasabian said simply.

"I beg your pardon? The what file?" Logan asked.

"The Tairge file," she repeated. "It was a channel of communication that Dr. Shaw and I used through the computer net when we had questions about certain things that might be going on. That's what the word tairge means—to question."

"How do you spell that?" Briscoe asked.

"T-A-I—"

"Hold it. You've gone far enough," Briscoe said. He looked over at Logan. "Are you thinking what I'm thinking?"

"Yeah. Maybe the T-A wasn't for Talbot. Maybe it was for this file. Maybe there was something in the file Shaw wanted us to see."

"Can we open this file?" Briscoe asked.

"Yes. I brought my laptop." She put the little computer on the desk, slipped the disk into the drive, then tapped a few keys. The screen filled with words, and she began moving the cursor through the copy, finally stopping.

"Here," she said, getting up. "Here is the last exchange we had. This was Wednesday afternoon, just after he found out about the report Dr. Corrigan was going to make to the shareholders. Go ahead and read it . . . use the cursor to move through. By the way, I am L, for Linda, Dr. Corrigan is D, for David, and Dr. Shaw is G, for Gary."

Logan sat down to the little computer, and

Briscoe moved into position to watch the screen over his shoulder.

Hi, L, have you got a minute? I want to ask you something.

Sure, what?

You're closer to D than I am. Does he have a wild hair up his ass today or is it just me?

It isn't just you. He's very nervous about the status report he's giving to the shareholders next week.

I don't blame him. When they find out what happened to batch 9384, they're going to be pretty upset. They might even pull the plug.

Oh, I hope not. If they pull the plug that will be the end of everything around here. We'll be out of a job!

Not to worry, my dear, D might not find as cushy a spot as he has now, but he'll land on his feet somewhere. We all will. Don't forget, I've got that offer from Chicago. If you'd like me to, I'll see that you get an interview with them too.

Thanks, but I'd rather stay here. Wouldn't you like to see us complete our work?

Of course. If I didn't feel that way, I would've already taken the Chicago position. But I don't see how we can continue here if our funding isn't renewed, and that's not likely to happen when they find out how far away we really are. Has D prepared the report yet?

Yes.

Have you read it?

Yes.

I'd sure like to see what he has to say.

It's in the Admin file. I don't think he's locked it, but he may have. I'm not sure D would want you to read it, though.

Why not?

I just think he would rather you not read it.

Now you've really got me curious. I think I'll just drop out for a few minutes and take a look at it.

I'm back! I can see why he wouldn't want me to read it. Can you believe that phony piece of shit D is submitting? He's using false data for the entire 9384 batch! Did you know he was going to do this?

Yes. He told me what he was going to do.

He sure as hell didn't say anything to me about it.

He knew you would disapprove.

You're damn right I disapprove. What about you, L? Didn't you tell him he was knowingly submitting faulty data?

I was more subtle with it, but I did remind him of the faulty test run with 9384.

What did he say?

He said the misinformation was only a matter of timing and was of no consequence to the final report anyway. He's going to issue a correction in a few weeks. He'll tell them that the 9384 charts are based upon an honest error made in the analysis recording. By that time the new funding will already be locked in and we can carry on our work.

This isn't right, L. If they can't trust him with that, how can they trust him with anything? He's going to cause the whole thing to blow up right in our faces. I'm going to have a talk with him.

I don't think you should.

Why not?

Because his mind is pretty well made up.

Then I'm going to do everything in my power to unmake it.

Logan tried to move the cursor down farther, but it was as far as it would go.

"That's the end of it," Dr. Kasabian said. "That was when he had his meeting with Dr. Corrigan. And, of course, I told you how that came out."

"We need to get Lieutenant Van Buren out here," Briscoe said, and went after her.

After explaining to the lieutenant how the computer files had been reconstructed, Briscoe invited her to peruse the two-way exchange between Dr. Kasabian and Dr. Shaw.

"Where did this particular file come from?" Van Buren asked Dr. Kasabian when she was finished.

"It was on the hard disk with the other files.

"You mean this exchange between you and Dr. Shaw was on every computer?" Van Buren asked.

"Yes."

"Then what would keep Dr. Corrigan . . . or anyone else with a computer station, from calling up your exchange and reading what you were talking about?"

"The Tairge file was a locked file. You had to type in the password 'Tairge' to open it. Gary and I were the only ones who knew the password. We could be talking back and forth right under everyone else's nose, and they would have no way of knowing," Dr. Kasabian said.

"Lennie, Mike, I want you to go down there and get a copy of everything that's on the computer files now."

"No, please, they can't do that," Dr. Kasabian said, holding up her hand as if to stop them. "The information on those files is all highly classified."

"Oh, we *can* do it, Doctor," Lieutenant Van Buren said. "It will take a judge's order, but we can do it."

"Then if you do, would you please guard it closely?"

"I thought you said you weren't really all that close to success," Briscoe said.

"We aren't."

"Then why so secretive about the information that's on there?" Briscoe asked.

"In research of this nature, information about failures can be just as valid as information about success. Anyway, just because we aren't as close to success as David says we are, doesn't mean that we haven't made a great deal of progress. I would say that we are years ahead of anyone else. It would be irresponsible not to take all precautions to safeguard it."

"It will be safeguarded," Van Buren promised. She looked over at Briscoe. "Sergeant, perhaps you had also better bring Dr. Corrigan in for a talk. And get a warrant to look through his house." She looked at Dr. Kasabian. "Doctor, thank you, very much, for bringing this to our attention."

"I . . . I do hope I did the right thing," Dr. Kasabian said.

LAW&
ORDER

Chapter
Seven

When Briscoe and Logan returned to Humaricare, they took a computer technician with them. As they stepped through the front door, the pretty young woman at the front desk looked up with a practiced smile.

"May I help you?" she asked.

"We'd like to speak to Dr. Corrigan," Briscoe said.

"I remember you. You're the police officers who were here earlier, aren't you? I'm sorry, Dr. Corrigan isn't in right now. Was he expecting you?"

"Not exactly," Briscoe said. He turned to the technician. "How about it, Danny? Do you need him here to do what you have to do?"

"No. All I need is a computer terminal," Danny replied.

"He has one in his office," Logan said, pointing toward a door.

"Let me take a look at it. If it's on-line with the others, I should be able to download everything I need right there."

The three men started for Corrigan's office, but the receptionist ran around to stand in front of them.

"Hold on!" she said. "What are you doing? You can't just barge in there like that!"

Logan showed her the warrant. "This says I can," he said.

"But Dr. Corrigan isn't here!"

"I suggest you do what you can to find him. Tell him we have a court order authorizing us to make a copy of everything that is on the Humaricare computer system."

The young woman gasped, then hurried back to her desk, where she frantically began to make a telephone call. She looked up just as Dr. Kasabian came out into the reception area.

"Oh, Dr. Kasabian, thank goodness you're here," the receptionist said, hanging up the phone. "These men—these police officers—are just barging right into Dr. Corrigan's office."

"Do you have court authorization to do this?" Dr. Kasabian asked calmly.

"Yes, right here," Briscoe said, showing it to her.

Dr. Kasabian held the paper for a moment as if studying it, then handed it back to Briscoe.

"It's all right, Judy," Dr. Kasabian said to the young woman. "The court has given them permission. There's nothing we can do about it."

"But what about David? Don't you think he should be told what's going on?"

"Do you know where he is?"

"He gave me a few numbers where he said he could be reached."

"Then by all means try to get hold of him," Dr. Kasabian said. "Tell him it might be a good idea for him to get down here."

Judy went back to her phone and began punching buttons. In the meantime, Dr. Kasabian followed the three men into Dr. Corrigan's office. She looked back toward Judy.

"You didn't say anything about my coming to see you, did you?" she asked anxiously. "I mean if word got out . . . it would be very uncomfortable for me around here."

"We haven't said anything yet," Briscoe replied. "But if anything comes from our investigation, you'll be called as a witness."

Dr. Kasabian bit her lower lip and nodded. "I realize that," she said. "If it goes that far, then I'm prepared to testify. But for now, at least, I can't believe David had anything to do with killing Gary, no matter what it looks like. I think I told you all this as much for my own peace of mind as anything else. I want to know that David didn't have anything to do with this."

Danny put his case down on the desk. "The disk in this hard drive is forty mb. Will that be enough, do you think?" he asked Dr. Kasabian. "If not, I have another one the same size."

"I should think that one would be enough," she said.

Danny connected his hard drive to the terminal, then sat down to the keyboard and began typing.

"I should probably tell you that several of the files are locked or copy protected," Dr. Kasabian offered.

"No problem," Danny replied. "I can get around that."

Logan chuckled as he watched Danny overcome the challenges the lab computer threw up. Within a moment he had information streaming from the computer onto his hard drive disk.

"I'm glad this guy is on our side," Logan said. "I'll just bet he could empty out a bank account in a moment with that thing."

"Don't think I'm not tempted to try it sometimes," Danny replied with a laugh.

For the next several minutes, while Danny sat at the keyboard, Briscoe and Logan searched through Dr. Corrigan's office, opening desk and filing cabinet drawers. They heard the front door open and Dr. Corrigan come into the building, then, an instant later, he burst into the office.

"What the hell is going on in here?" he demanded angrily. "What are you doing in my desk? Get out of it." When he saw Dr. Kasabian, he turned his anger toward her. "Dr. Kasabian, did you give these men permission to come in here like this?"

"They didn't need to ask for my permission," Dr. Kasabian replied. "They already had it." She showed Corrigan the court order, and he read through it for a moment, his face growing redder and his temple pounding in anger.

"All right," he finally said. "So you have permission to rifle through my desk drawers, but who is that person and what is he doing at the computer?"

"His name is Daniel Graves, and he's downloading all of your computer files," Logan explained. "It's part of our investigation into the shooting death of Dr. Shaw."

"The information in those files is classified!" Dr. Corrigan said. "I don't see what that could possibly have to do with the investigation of a murder."

"Judge Waters feels differently," Logan said. "He signed the warrant."

"Hey, Mike, look at this," Briscoe said, holding up a slip of paper. "It's a gun permit . . . a P-38, serial number 7812. Registered to one David Corrigan."

"Do you own a P-38, nine millimeter pistol, Dr. Corrigan?" Logan asked.

"Yes, of course I own one. That permit gives me permission, I believe. Unless you are going to charge me with that as well."

"Do you know where that pistol is?"

"What do you mean? Why are you asking me? It's right there in the drawer, with the permit."

Logan looked in the drawer again. "It isn't here," he said.

"But of course it is. Look again."

Logan looked again. "No, it isn't here."

"Don't be ridiculous. I always keep the gun and the permit together," Dr. Corrigan said. He moved over to the desk and began searching. "It's here somewhere. It has to be," he said anxiously.

"What do you mean, you did own one?"

"When is the last time you saw it?"

"I don't know," Corrigan answered. He rifled through all the drawers. "I can't remember. I—I'm not exactly what you would call a gun enthusiast. I've never shot it, nor do I ever wish to shoot it. I bought it last year when there was a rash of break-ins in my apartment building. I put it away in the drawer and never paid any attention to it again." He stood up and shrugged. "It doesn't matter. I figure it's good riddance."

"Dr. Corrigan, are you saying you have no idea what happened to it?" Briscoe asked.

"That's what I'm saying. Anyway, what difference does it make? Why is it so important?"

"Because it was a nine millimeter pistol that killed Dr. Shaw."

"A nine millimeter? What does that have to do with me?"

"A P-38 is a nine millimeter," Briscoe said. "Your gun, the one you say is now missing, is a nine millimeter."

Corrigan's face went white and he took a couple of steps backward. "Oh my God," he said. "Do you suppose my gun could actually be the cause of Gary's death." He sat down, then leaned his head forward, propping it up on his elbow. "How horrible that would be."

"Dr. Corrigan, I think you had better come down to the station with us. We'd like to ask you a few questions."

"All right," he said. "Yes, maybe it would be best if we did get all this straightened out. I, uh, do you mind if I call my lawyer?"

"I think that would be an excellent idea," Briscoe replied.

* * *

While they were waiting for Corrigan's lawyer to arrive, Briscoe and Logan took a search warrant out to Corrigan's apartment, where they had a look around.

"You don't really think the gun will be here, do you?" Logan asked as he and Briscoe rummaged through drawers and shelves.

"It would be nice, wouldn't it?" Briscoe replied, running his hands down inside the cushioned sofa. "Or, barring that, maybe a signed confession that says 'I killed Shaw.' "

Logan chuckled. "Yeah, I could handle that," he said. He picked up the trash can and looked inside. "Well now, what have we here?"

"What have you found?" Briscoe asked. He finished with the sofa, then began sticking his hands down behind the cushion of the chair.

Logan stuck his hand down into the wastebasket and brought up a tiny tape cassette. He held it up for Briscoe to see.

"It's a tape from an answering machine," he said.

"Let's play it," Briscoe suggested.

Logan walked over to the answering machine and looked at it. "That's funny," he said.

"What?"

"He took the old tape out, but he didn't put a new one in." Logan put the tape in the machine, rewound it, then began playing the messages back. There were a few incidental messages, one from the Columbia University Alumni Association, one trying to sell magazines, then they recognized Dr. Kasabian's voice.

"David, this is Linda. It's ten-thirty, Wednesday night, and I just spoke with Gary. He's still down at the office. He's very upset about the report you're going to give at the meeting Friday. I really think you need to talk to him. I think you should go down there tonight."

Then they heard a message from Dr. Shaw. It gave them each an eerie feeling, as if someone were talking to them from beyond the grave.

"David, uh, I'm down at the office. If it's not asking too much, I'd like to talk to you. Are you there? Come on, I know you're there. Pick up the phone, damn it."

"What is it, Gary? What's wrong?"

"What's wrong? You know damn well what's wrong. We need—"

The tape stopped at that point.

"What do you think?" Logan asked.

"I think Dr. Corrigan has just moved to number one on our list of suspects."

Interrogation Room A

When Briscoe and Logan returned to the station, they looked through the one-way glass into the interrogation room. Dr. Corrigan was already inside, sitting at the table beside his lawyer. The lawyer, a tall, thin man, with curly white hair, was talking, and Dr. Corrigan was listening intently.

"Are you ready to go in?" Briscoe asked.

"Let's do it," Logan replied.

When they entered the interrogation room, Corrigan's lawyer stood, but Dr. Corrigan remained seated.

"Gentleman, I'm Thurman Moore, Dr. Corrigan's attorney," he said. "May I ask if charges are being filed against my client?"

"I won't kid around with you, Mr. Moore," Briscoe replied. "Charges are being filed, yes. Murder two."

Moore sat back down then looked at the two police officers as if he couldn't believe what he was hearing.

"Murder two?" he asked quietly. "Dr. Corrigan is one of the most respected research physicians in the nation. In the world. You can't be serious with this charge! What earthly reason would he have to murder a colleague?"

"I'm afraid we are very serious," Briscoe said. "Dr. Corrigan, we read you your rights when we questioned you the first time. If you like, we can read them again."

Corrigan waved his hand impatiently. "Never mind," he said. "I don't have to have everything explained to me like some hoodlum you've picked up at the bus station."

"So was Gary Shaw. Did you kill Gary Shaw?"

"No, I did not kill Dr. Shaw. Dr. Shaw was not only a colleague, he was a dear friend. Why would I want to kill him?"

"That's a good question," Moore said. "Why would David want to kill Dr. Shaw?"

"Maybe there was a difference of opinion between them on how the research was going," Logan suggested.

Dr. Corrigan laughed dryly. "Really? And where did you study medicine, officer? You couldn't explain the simplest formula in the equation, how would you know whether we were having a difference of opinion or not?"

"I may not understand chemistry or physics, Doctor, but I do understand ethics and morality," Logan replied. "Perhaps that is where you and Dr. Shaw were having a difference of opinion."

"Oh, my God," Moore said, slapping the table and leaning forward. "You're a right-to-lifer, aren't you? That's where all this is going!

You are passing judgment on the ethics and morality of Dr. Corrigan's work."

"What? Where did you get such an idea?" Logan replied, shocked by Moore's reaction.

"Dr. Corrigan, I advise you to make no further statement at this time," Moore said. He smiled at Logan and Briscoe. "Take it to court if you wish. We'll throw your right-to-life ideas right back in your face."

Office of the District Attorney

"I'm sorry," Logan said. He was sitting on the sofa in Wentworth's office, pinching the bridge of his nose as he finished explaining the scene in the interrogation room. "I guess I wasn't thinking when I brought up the ethics thing."

"What on earth made you say a thing like that in the first place?" Claire asked. "Ethics? Morality? Don't you realize those are buzz words that swarm around the whole issue of abortion?"

"Come on, Claire, ease up a little," Stone said. "You know he wasn't referring to the ethics of the research."

"Yes, I know it. But Moore is going to have a field day with it."

"Maybe not," Wentworth said. The D.A. was sitting behind his desk with his hands folded across his chest.

"You have an idea, Adam?" Stone asked.

"Not an idea, exactly," Wentworth replied. "I'd call it more of a notion."

"What is it?"

"Claire is right when she says words like ethics and morality are buzz words in a case like this. But buzz words, like a buzz saw, cuts both ways."

"What do you mean?" Claire asked.

"Don't you think there's a possibility that if Moore tries to make too much of the ethics and morality issue, it might just backfire on him? It might cause some people to start thinking about things that they haven't thought about before."

"You mean some people who have never considered themselves either pro-choice or pro-life might suddenly have to make the decision?" Logan asked.

"Precisely." Wentworth replied. "It might open a crap game that Moore would just as soon not play."

Logan smiled. "Yeah," he said. "Yeah, it might. At least, I hope so."

"Now, what's the latest with Alfusco?" Wentworth asked. "Will he be a witness for us?"

Stone nodded. "I talked to him and he ac-

cepted our offer. He will testify in return for a
suspended sentence on the charge of malicious
break-in.''

"And Dr. Kasabian?''

"I talked to her again this morning," Claire
said. "She's ready. She's going to be a dynamite
witness. As a matter of fact, she's practically our
entire case.''

Wentworth drummed his fingers on the desk
for a long, silent moment. When Stone started
to say something, Wentworth held up his finger
to stop him. The silent moment stretched on.

"Adam, is something wrong?" Stone finally
asked.

"Suppose, for some reason, we couldn't use
Kasabian's testimony," he asked.

Claire laughed nervously. "What do you
mean? Why couldn't we use it?''

"I don't know. Maybe she gets hit by a car on
her way to court. Maybe she's suddenly struck
mute. Come up with your own scenario. The
question is, can we make this case without her
testimony?''

"No," Claire said. "I don't think we can.''
She had a confused look on her face. "But why
should we?''

Wentworth smiled, and the tension was broken. "You're right," he replied. "Why should
we?''

"What about bail?" Stone asked.

"I don't think he's a runner," Wentworth said. "But I do want him to feel some pressure. Ask for a million. If we get half that, I'll be satisfied."

Superior Court, October 4

Judge Amon Heckemeyer sat Buddhalike on the bench while Thurman Moore questioned the prospective jurors.

A middle-aged Caucasian female was being questioned.

"Mrs. Kirby, if you had to describe yourself, would you say you are pro-life or pro-choice?" Moore asked.

"I've never really given it any particular thought," the middle-aged woman replied.

"Oh come now, Mrs. Kirby," Moore replied. "The abortion issue is one of the hottest issues in the country now. It's the pivotal issue in some elections. Nominees for the Supreme Court are given litmus tests to see how they stand on it. Yet you say you have no thought on it one way or the other."

"Why should I have any thought about it? As you can see, I am obviously beyond child-bearing age," Mrs. Kirby replied. "The question of abortion is not something I will ever have to face."

"You may face it sooner than you think," Moore said. "We are trying a man for murder. It just so happens that this man is also working on an abortion pill. You are, no doubt, going to hear testimony about abortion. Some people consider abortion murder. Those same people might also believe that anyone who commits an abortion would be capable of committing murder. Do you consider abortion murder?"

"No. Not unless the baby could survive outside the womb."

"Your Honor, strike for cause," Moore said, turning toward the bench.

"I beg your pardon?" the judge replied in surprise. "The answer I just heard was that she does not consider abortion murder."

"It was the use of the word baby, Your Honor. Referring to a fetus as a baby loads the issue and is highly prejudicial."

Judge Heckemeyer sighed. "Very well, you are excused, Mrs. Kirby. Mr. Moore, you aren't going to hold out for a jury composed entirely of pro-choice activists, are you?"

"Not necessarily, but I do want a level playing field."

The next prospective juror took his seat. Moore studied his sheet of paper for a moment, then looked up at the man.

"What is your religion, Mr. Phillips?"

"Roman Catholic," Phillips replied.

"Move to strike, Your Honor."

"For what reason?"

"He is Roman Catholic, Your Honor. The Roman Catholic Church is known to have a very strong bias against abortion."

"Mr. Moore, I am Baptist," Judge Heckemeyer said. "The Baptist also have a very strong bias against abortion, are you aware of that?"

Moore was silent for a long moment. "Yes, sir, I am aware," he finally answered.

"Then why haven't you challenged me, Mr. Moore?" Judge Heckemeyer asked.

"Your Honor, I don't think a challenge is necessary."

"Oh? Why not? How is it that you can take one look at Mr. Phillips and decide that he will be influenced by his religion, whereas I won't be? Should I be flattered that you respect my ability to disregard personal prejudices? Or should I be insulted because you might feel that I lack a personal conviction? Is that it, Mr. Moore? Do you feel that Mr. Phillips is a better Catholic than I am a Baptist?"

"I hardly think so, Your Honor," Moore said, pulling his collar away from his neck with his finger. "Actually, I don't know you or Mr. Phillips well enough to form an opinion one way or the other.''

"And yet you have just challenged Mr. Phillips purely on the basis of his religion. Tell me, Mr. Moore, were you going to wait until the trial was over, then challenge me if it didn't turn out your way?''

"No, Your Honor," Moore said quickly, so quickly that Stone realized that that was exactly what Moore planned to do.

"You may continue to question the juror, Mr. Moore. If you can find cause for striking him, other than the fact that he happens to be Catholic, then I will allow you to do so. Otherwise, he stands.''

"Yes, sir," Moore said.

Moore questioned the prospective juror for a few minutes longer. The juror said that while he was opposed to abortion and would strongly counsel anyone seeking his advice against abortion, he did not feel that his view would color his ability to make a decision as to the guilt or innocence of Dr. Corrigan.

Moore paused for a long moment, then accepted him.

Stone wrote a note on the yellow tablet, then turned it so that Claire could see it.

"One for our side. If he hadn't had the run-in with the judge, he would've struck this one, and the judge would've allowed it.''

"What do you mean 'our' side?" Claire wrote back. "I hope I don't have to climb into bed with a lot of rabid pro-lifers."

"Climb into bed? Interesting metaphor," Stone wrote back, laughing quietly.

Quickly, Claire drew a picture of a pig, then beneath it wrote the words "male chauvinist," then "Ben Stone." She drew an arrow from the name, pointing to the pig. When she showed it to Stone, he laughed again.

Jury selection continued for the rest of the day, finally ending at just before five. Judge Heckemeyer then recessed the court until the following day.

Channel surfing with one hand and eating a tuna fish sandwich with the other, Claire Kincaid was looking for a news show when she suddenly saw Dr. Corrigan's picture on the screen. Because it wasn't one of the channels she normally watched, she stopped to see what this was about. Dr. Corrigan's picture disappeared, replaced by a studio set consisting of a semicircular desk, around which sat three men.

"Hello, I'm Brook Lee, and this is Spectrum. *The entire nation will be watching the trial of Dr. David Corrigan, accused of murdering a colleague, Dr. Gary Shaw.*

"Dr. Corrigan and Dr. Shaw were working on the controversial PEBC, a birth control pill which could

*be taken within the first forty-eight hours after inter-
course. If, during that forty-eight-hour period of time,
conception has occurred, the PEBC could interrupt
the process. Because of that, some call it an abortion
pill, not too dissimilar to RU 486, the abortion pill
developed by a French physician. We'll be back after
these messages."*

While the TV station ran commercials for var-
ious products, Claire called Ben Stone.

"Ben," she said when he answered. "Are you
watching *Spectrum*?"

"Yes," Stone replied.

"What do you think? Good for us, or bad?"

"Depends on what you're looking for,"
Stone said.

"What do you mean?"

"If you're looking for publicity, then this is
going to be right down your alley. But if you're
looking for it to help our case, you can think
again."

"They're coming back," Claire said, and
hung up the phone.

"Let's identify the issue, ladies and gentlemen,"
Brook Lee said. *"Dr. David Corrigan, a researcher
working on an abortion pill, is being tried for the
murder of a colleague. But is that the real issue? My
guests today don't think so. But that is the only thing
on which they agree. On my left, meet Mason Alexander, spokesman—"*

"I prefer the term spokesperson," Alexander interrupted.

"Very well, so as not to offend anyone, we will call you spokesperson. And you are a spokesperson for America Forward? A pro-abortion advocate?"

Alexander held up his hand. *"Again, we're dealing with semantics here. But in a case as fraught with emotion as this one is, I think we do ourselves no service by misapplying the labels. Therefore, I prefer to be promoted as being representative of pro-choice, not pro abortion."*

"Bear with me, Mr. Alexander, I'll get it right," Lee said. *"And now, on my right, Dexter Keene, spokesman . . . or rather, spokesperson for the ACLW, and that is Action Committee for Life Watch. Did I get that right, Mr. Keene?"*

"Yes, but I don't mind being called a spokesman. We at ACLW recognize that there is a difference between men and women, and we celebrate that difference."

"You don't celebrate women, you put them down," Alexander said.

"We do not put them down, sir. On the contrary, we revere them for the nobility of their sex. When did it become wrong to—"

"Wait a minute, wait a minute," Lee said, breaking into the conversation. *"I feel like the referee at a basketball game that started before the toss-up. Now, if you are each going to make your point, we're going to have to have some order here. And since it is my*

show," Lee smiled at the camera, *"I am the one who establishes this order. Mr. Keene, what do you think about the trial of Dr. Corrigan? Do you feel he will be able to get a fair trial?"*

"No."

"Well, on that issue we certainly agree," Alexander said. *"I don't think he will get a fair trial either."*

"Very well, let us start from that reference point," Lee said. *"Mr. Keene, why do you think he won't get a fair trial?"*

"Because he isn't being tried for what he should be tried for," Keene said. *"He is being tried for the murder of a colleague . . . another doctor who, like Dr. Corrigan, was working to develop an abortion pill. If this were going to be a fair trial, Corrigan would be tried for attempting to develop a method of slaughter of as many as one million babies every year."*

"What?" Alexander shouted. *"Have you lost your mind?"*

"Do you dispute that?" Keene shot back.

"Of course I dispute it!"

"I didn't just pull those numbers out of the air, Mr. Alexander," Keene said. *"The estimate comes from a well-respected survey, contracted for by a major pharmaceutical industry."*

"Good point," Lee said. *"What do you have to say about that, Mr. Alexander? Those are awfully impressive numbers."*

"In the first place, that is the high side of the high-

est set of numbers I've heard," Alexander replied. *"But more than the numbers, I dispute the very concept of 'slaughtering babies.' This pill, if it is developed, would do no such thing. It is a post-event birth control pill. It stops the activity of conception, which —if allowed to continue—would eventually develop into a fetus. And the fetus, if brought to full term and delivered, becomes a baby."*

"Are you saying now that a fetus must go full term before it can be classified as a baby?" Keene asked. *"What about premature births? My oldest daughter was two months premature. She is now a high school cheerleader. Are you trying to make me believe that she is, somehow, less than the others on her cheering squad, because she was born two months early?"*

"That is not what I'm saying and you know it," Alexander said. He turned to Brook Lee. *"And that is why it's going to be impossible to have a fair trial for Dr. Corrigan. Because the real issue—did he or did he not murder Dr. Shaw—is going to be lost in all the rhetoric of such fire-breathers as Mr. Dexter Keene and the Action Committee for Life Watch."*

"Don't go away, folks. We'll be right back," Lee said.

Claire did exactly what Brook Lee didn't want her to do. She went away, choosing to turn the set off entirely, rather than watch the news.

She had wanted this case, and had gone to Ben to plead with him to make certain they drew it. She had properly guessed that it would be a high-profile case. But now she was having second thoughts.

It was high profile, true enough, but it brought its own baggage to court. It was so loaded with issues that had nothing to do with the central point that Claire was beginning to fear they would never get to the issues. Seating the jury today had been a perfect example of what they were faced with. Very few of the normal questions surrounding such a case were asked. Moore didn't seem to care whether or not any of the prospective jurors had preconceived opinions as to Corrigan's guilt or innocence. All he wanted to know about was their opinion on abortion.

The idiots on TV were right. There was no way that question wasn't going to be a major part of the trial. And with a question that big, the issue of guilt or innocence as to the murder of Dr. Shaw was likely to be almost a second thought. And the prosecutors who tried the case would be lost in the shuffle.

Chapter Eight

Superior Court of New York

The demonstrators were out in full force as Stone and Kincaid arrived for the trial. The police had set up barricade lines of yellow plastic tape beyond which the pro-lifers, on one side, and the pro-choice activists, on the other, could not advance. If they couldn't advance physically beyond the barricade, they were determined to make up for it with increased volume, for the passionately committed on both sides were almost hysterical in their shouting match.

"They're turning this entire thing into a circus," Claire said as she and Ben Stone stepped inside, away from the crowd. "How will we ever manage to get to the issue at hand if they interfere with the process?"

157

Stone chuckled. "This *is* the process, counselor," he said. "Or haven't you learned that yet?"

They passed through a metal detector, then went upstairs into a small ready room that they could use while they were waiting for their case to be called. Stone sat down at the table, but Claire walked over to look out the window. A pigeon landed on the ledge just on the other side of the windowpane, and he stared through the glass at Claire, totally unafraid, as if aware of the presence of the glass between them. His legs were ruby red, his body gray, and his eyes small and beady. Claire looked back at him.

"Are you ready? Or do you want to go through it one time?" Stone asked.

Claire turned back toward him. "I beg your pardon?"

"Your opening statement," Stone said. "Are you ready to give it?"

"Yes. I rehearsed several times last night. I'm as ready as I'll ever be."

"Are you sure you don't want to go through it one last time?"

"No. I've got a good edge on now. If I go through it, I may lose some of that edge."

Stone chuckled. "Spoken like a true showman," he said.

Someone knocked lightly on the door, then pushed it open. "Mr. Kincaid?"

"I'm Miss Kincaid," Claire answered.

The courtroom messenger blushed. "I beg your pardon, it didn't say," he explained. "It just says that Kincaid will be presenting the opening argument for the prosecution."

"That's right, that's me. What can I do for you?"

"I thought I'd tell you in case you want to go on into the courtroom. Judge Heckemeyer will be taking his seat in about five minutes."

"Thank you," Claire replied. She turned toward Stone, then brushed the front of her dress. "How do I look?" she asked. "All right?"

"You look very nice," Stone replied, not sure what he was supposed to say. "Very pretty."

Claire dismissed his response with an impatient wave of her hand. "I don't mean that," she said. "I mean do I look too young? I don't want to look too young. I want to make a very professional appearance."

"You look cool and poised," Stone said. It was the right thing to say, because Claire relaxed visibly.

They walked from the little anteroom to the courtroom, then took their place at the prosecutor's table. Dr. Corrigan and his attorney were already sitting at the defense table.

The trial had attracted a great deal of attention, so the courtroom was filled to capacity. As Stone looked out over the gallery, he saw Dr.

Kasabian; Judy, the receptionist from Humaricare; and one or two others whom he had met down at the clinic. He also saw Jerry Talbot and Paul Alfusco. Both men had been served with subpoenas to testify for the prosecution.

"All rise!" the bailiff said, and Stone looked back toward the front as Judge Heckemeyer came into the room. Heckemeyer sat down at his bench, then rapped once, with his gavel.

"Call the case," he said.

"Case number 930913, State of New York verses David R. Corrigan. The charge is Murder in the Second Degree," the bailiff read.

"Is the defendant in the court?"

Thurman Moore, the defense counsel, stood. "Defense is present, Your Honor, and represented by counsel."

"Is Defense ready to present its case?" Judge Heckemeyer asked.

"Defense is ready, Your Honor."

Judge Heckemeyer looked over at the prosecutor's table.

"Is the State ready?"

"Prosecution is ready, Your Honor," Claire answered.

"Very well, the State may present its opening statement."

Claire stood up and walked over to look at the jury that had been selected. On the whole, she was fairly pleased with the jury makeup.

The obvious right-to-lifers, those who wore their cause on their sleeve, had been excused for cause. Though they might have been a bit more prone to find for the prosecution, Claire was just as glad they had been excused. She preferred to deal with people who would make their decision based upon a fair hearing and reasonable judgment of the case presented, rather than base it upon a prejudice against the work Dr. Corrigan was doing.

There were six women on the jury. There were two blacks, one Hispanic, and one Asian. The mean educational level of the jury was thirteen and one-half years. They were what the jury system was supposed to be, a panel of ordinary citizens, drawn together to perform an extraordinary task. They would decide upon the guilt or innocence of Dr. David Corrigan, and their decision could set him free or end his career and send him to prison.

Claire began speaking quietly, and the jury, almost as one, leaned forward attentively to listen. This was exactly what she wanted, and as they leaned forward, she raised her voice slightly.

"Ladies and gentlemen of the jury, I am sure you know by now, for there is no way you could not know unless you have been on Mars, or lost in the jungles of the Amazon, that Dr. David Corrigan is a research physician. Dr. Corrigan's particular field of interest has been, for some time, the development of an abortion pill.

"Because of the controversial nature of that work, there are many Americans of good conscience and sincere belief who are unable to separate David Corrigan the man from Dr. David Corrigan the noted researcher. He is in one of those professions where the profession becomes bigger than the individual. Those whose personal beliefs are such that they feel Dr. Corrigan would be doing the world a great service by successfully developing a safe abortion pill, may tend to let that cloud the issue at hand. By the same token, those people whose personal beliefs tend toward regarding abortion as something wrong, will allow their prejudice to cloud the issue at hand. And that would be too bad, for we must not lose sight of the issue at hand.

"What *is* the issue at hand?

"The issue is murder. Dr. Corrigan murdered Dr. Shaw. The motive for this murder was greed . . . greed for money, greed for power, and greed for prestige.

"In his position as director and chief research physician at Humaricare, development of a safe and easy-to-use abortion pill would bring Dr. Corrigan the money, power, and prestige that he seeks." Claire paused, then looked back toward Dr. Corrigan. He was looking at the table and made no effort to meet her gaze.

"Dr. Corrigan has not yet discovered the formula he needs to make the abortion pill a reality. But he has discovered something else just as important. He has discovered that if he can make people believe that success is imminent, then the perks are just as great.

"If he is close to success, almost unlimited funding continues, Dr. Corrigan's name remains in the forefront in the medical research world, and he is invited to give lectures, write articles, and receive rewards. All this, only because he is perceived to be close to success.

"But, as the State will prove, Dr. Corrigan is *not* close to success.

"The State will prove this. The State will also prove that in order to keep the funding and other perks going, Dr. Corrigan began lying about the progress of his research progress. He issued doctored reports to give the impression that Humaricare was just on the verge of a great breakthrough."

Claire paused for a long moment to let that thought sink in, studying the effect it had on Dr. Corrigan, who showed no reaction at all.

Claire then turned back toward the jury to continue her opening presentation.

"Unfortunately for Dr. Corrigan, Dr. Gary Shaw not only knew that the information being put out by Dr. Corrigan was wrong . . . he also believed it to be unethical. Dr. Shaw confronted Dr. Corrigan with what he knew, then he made a fatal mistake. Hoping to force Dr. Corrigan to do the right thing, Dr. Shaw gave him an ultimatum. Either Dr. Corrigan would withdraw his false reports, or Dr. Shaw would, personally, discredit them.

"The State believes that Dr. Shaw then became a threat to Dr. Corrigan. If it became known by his financial backers and others how far Humaricare really was from developing the abortion pill, Dr. Corrigan would lose the three things that had become so important to him: money, power, and prestige. He could not let that happen, so he stopped Dr. Shaw in the most effective way he could. He killed Gary Shaw by firing a pistol bullet into his heart.

"The bullet that killed Dr. Gary Shaw was a nine millimeter bullet. We believe there is some significance to this, because a nine millimeter pistol is rather distinctive among handguns. Unlike .22, .32, and .38 caliber pistols, the nine millimeter is not readily available as 'Saturday night specials.' Nine millimeter pistols are generally more expensive weapons, not the kind of gun your average break-in specialist would own."

Claire stopped for a long moment and stared over at the defense table. "Dr. Corrigan owns such a gun, though. We will present official documents showing that Dr. Corrigan has bought and registered a P-38, nine millimeter pistol. Unfortunately, we do not have the pistol because Dr. Corrigan has 'lost' it. I think it should be pointed out, however, that no missing weapon report was ever filed, because Dr. Corrigan didn't lose the pistol until 'after' Dr. Shaw was murdered.''

Claire stood there a moment longer, then returned to her seat at the prosecutor's table.

''Good job,'' Stone whispered.

''Mr. Moore, opening statement?'' Judge Heckemeyer asked.

''Yes, Your Honor. Allow me one moment please.'' Moore made a last minute consultation with Dr. Corrigan, then stood up. Clearing his throat and adjusting his tie, he walked over to stand in front of the jury box.

''Money, power, and prestige,'' Moore began, counting them off on his fingers. He stopped and looked over at the prosecutor's table. ''Miss Kincaid spoke those words as if they were something vile . . . something to be eschewed. She would have us believe that only the most evil people would actively seek money, power, and prestige. And yet, I ask you this. Is there even one among you who would not accept money, power, or prestige if it were fairly and honestly offered? Is the fair and honest pursuit of money, power, and prestige not the 'Great American Dream'?

"I'll answer that question for you. It *is* the Great American Dream. Money, power, and prestige is not, of itself, evil. But I will admit that it does generate a great deal of emotion. And the emotion it generates does often get in the way of judgment, common sense, and even truth. What is it Miss Kincaid said? Oh, yes, she said 'We must not lose sight of the issue.' And then, having said that, she undertook in every way she could to cloud the issue with such emotion-packed concepts as abortion, money, power, prestige, and greed.

"Why does the State feel it is necessary to obfuscate the facts with emotion? The answer is simple." Moore raised his hand and wagged his finger back and forth. "They don't have the facts on their side.

"Oh, they have the bullet, and a lab test which connects the fatal bullet to a cartridge that they found. They also have the registration which proves that Dr. Corrigan owned a nine millimeter pistol. We will admit that. Dr. Corrigan did own a nine millimeter pistol, and that is the caliber pistol that was used to shoot Dr. Shaw. But let me tell you what they do not have. They do not have anything that proves it was Dr. Corrigan's gun that killed Dr. Shaw. And even if they did, there is no proof that Dr. Corrigan pulled the trigger. Anyone can shoot a gun. You don't have to buy it and register it to shoot it. Shooting a gun is as easy as wiggling your finger.''

Moore held his hand out, crooked as if he were grasping a pistol. He curled his forefinger back as if pulling a trigger.

''Who was it? Who shot the gun that killed Dr. Shaw?''

''If you think about it, anyone who knew he kept the gun there could be the guilty party. Likewise anyone who might have broken into the building that night for . . . oh, I don't know, let's take a wild flight of fancy and say they wanted to put up a poster, or destroy files, or purge computers . . . might easily have found the gun and committed the murder. A moment ago I told you that the prosecution had the fatal bullet, and the shell casing from which the bullet came. Now I am going to tell you where they found that empty shell casing. They found it in Mr. Paul Alfusco's apartment.

''Who is Paul Alfusco, you ask?'' Moore held up his finger. ''Prosecution is going to introduce two witnesses who will admit that they did, in fact, break into the office that night. One of the two is Paul Alfusco. Now, I'm not saying they are the ones who killed Dr. Shaw, you understand. That's not my job. I do not have to prove who *did* do it. All we have to do is show you that the possibility does exist for someone else to be guilty. And, if there is the *slightest* chance that anyone else did do it, then that leaves a reasonable doubt that Dr. Corrigan did *not* do it." Moore smiled, then held up both hands. "And we all know what that means, don't we, ladies and gentlemen? If there is the slightest doubt in your mind that Dr. Corrigan did it, then you must find Dr. Corrigan not guilty."

When Moore returned to his seat, Dr. Corrigan stood up to shake his hand. Claire was watching the jury, and she noticed that several people were nodding affirmatively.

"Oh," she said softly.

"What is it?"

"Look at the jury. They bought everything he said, hook, line, and sinker."

"I don't blame them. It was a very good opening statement," Stone replied.

"Ben," Claire said, almost in a hurt tone of voice.

Stone chuckled. "Hey, come on, I didn't say it was better than yours. I just said it was good. It was, wasn't it?"

"Yes," Claire agreed.

"Listen, I don't mind losing a case now and again," Stone said. "But I don't ever want to lose one because I have underestimated the opposition. Anyone who would do that deserves to lose."

Claire smiled. "You're right," she replied.

"The ball is in our court," Stone said. "Let's play."

Judge Heckemeyer studied a piece of paper on his desk for a long moment, then looked up and cleared his throat. "Prosecution may call the first witness," he said.

Stone stood up. "Your Honor, the State calls Don Forbes to the stand," Stone said.

Don Forbes was sworn in and took the stand. He identified himself as an employee of the Busy Bee Cleaning Service. He testified that he and his partner, Tony Bolino, arrived at the Humaricare office shortly before seven o'clock on the morning of the eleventh of August, to do their regular cleaning. They found the front window smashed, papers strewn all over the floor, and an anti-abortion poster pinned to the wall.

"What did you do when you made that discovery?"

"We tried to call Dr. Shaw at his home, but we got no answer. We didn't know it at the time, but he was already dead. Then we called the police."

"What did you do then?"

"Nothin'. We didn't do nothin'. We sort of figured that the best thing to do would be just wait around till the police got there. We figured that if we touched anything it might . . . you know, leave our fingerprints there or somethin'."

"But you did touch the phone?"

"Oh, yeah, we done that. I mean I touched one of 'em, and Tony, he touched the other one. But we didn't touch nothin' else."

"When did you discover the body?"

"Actually, we didn't discover it. We didn' know nothin' about Dr. Shaw bein' dead till the two policemen came. They the ones discovered it."

"Thank you, Mr. Forbes. No further questions."

Moore stood up. "Mr. Forbes, did you attempt to call Dr. Corrigan?"

"No, sir."

"So, you would have no way of knowing whether or not he was home that morning."

"No, sir."

"Why didn't you call him? He is the director, is he not? Wouldn't he be the logical person to call?"

"Yes, sir, I guess so, but Dr. Shaw was always easier to talk to."

"Why was that? Was Dr. Corrigan rude or unpleasant with you?"

"No, sir, it wasn't nothin' like that. Dr. Corrigan just always seemed, you know, too busy. Me an' Tony didn't like to bother him. It seemed like Dr. Shaw was easier to talk to."

"Thank you, no further questions," Moore said.

William Milsap, the ranking officer of the two police officers who answered the first call, also testified, sometimes referring to his notebooks to get certain facts straight.

"Officer Milsap, what was the position of the body when you found it?" Stone asked.

"He was sitting in his chair, slumped over on his desk," Milsap said, demonstrating by leaning forward.

Milsap went on to say that he observed a bullet hole in Dr. Shaw's chest.

"It was easy to see," he said.

"Why was that?"

"Well, he was wearing one of those white coats, lab coats I think they're called. And the bullet hole showed up quite clearly. There was also blood on the desk where he had been lying."

"Did you discover anything else with the body?"

"Yes, sir. There was a tablet beside him, and he had written the letters T-A—"

"Objection, Your Honor. It has not been established for certain that Dr. Shaw is the one who wrote the letters T-A."

"Is that right?" Judge Heckemeyer asked Stone.

"We've had two handwriting experts examine it, Your Honor," Stone replied. "One believes Dr. Shaw did write the note, the other thinks there may be some doubt."

Heckemeyer rubbed his chin for a moment, then cleared his throat. He leaned back in his chair. "The objection is sustained. Strike the statement as to who wrote the note."

"Did you find the murder weapon?"

"No, sir, I did not."

"Did you find an empty shell casing?"

"No, sir, I did not."

"Thank you. No further questions."

Moore stood up and walked toward the witness chair.

"Officer Milsap, when you arrived at the clinic, did you see any sign of forced entry?"

"The front window was broken out," Milsap said.

"As an act of vandalism, or for forced entry?"

"I have no way of actually knowing that," Milsap said.

"Other than the broken window, were there any other signs of vandalism?"

"Yes, sir."

"Would you describe them please?"

"The file cabinets were all open and files

were scattered all over the floor. There was also a poster on the wall."

"Would you describe that poster, please?"

"It was of a pregnant woman, holding a gun to her abdomen. The caption read, 'If you must abort your baby, try this!' "

Moore walked over to the evidence table and picked up a poster. "Is this the poster?"

"Yes, sir."

"Thank you. I am through with this witness, Your Honor."

Officer Milsap was followed by Sergeant Lennie Briscoe.

Briscoe testified that he and his partner, Officer Mike Logan, had found the registration paper, showing that Dr. Corrigan owned a P-38 pistol, which, Briscoe pointed out, used nine millimeter cartridges. He also testified that they had found an answering machine tape in Corrigan's home, on which there were recorded messages of Dr. Kasabian, and then Dr. Shaw calling Dr. Corrigan, asking him to come down to the clinic. The message from Dr. Shaw was answered by Corrigan, though the answer was incomplete.

"Do you know when the messages were recorded?" Claire asked.

"Yes," Briscoe replied. "Dr. Kasabian's message was recorded at ten-thirty on the night Dr. Shaw was killed. Dr. Shaw's message was sometime after that, we don't know when. It had to be on the same night, however, for Dr. Shaw was discovered dead the next morning.''

The tape was played for the benefit of the jury.

''Thank you, Sergeant Briscoe. I have no further questions.''

''Sergeant Briscoe,'' Moore began, on redirect, ''on the tape you just played, the reply from Dr. Corrigan was incomplete, wasn't it?''

''Yes, sir.''

''So, just by listening to that tape, we would have no way of knowing whether Dr. Corrigan went down to see Dr. Shaw or not, would we?''

''No, sir, but the tape was found in the trash can, as if he were trying to get rid of it before it came to light.''

''It could also mean that the tape was so badly worn he was replacing it with a new one, couldn't it?'' Moore asked. ''You don't have to answer, Sergeant. The answer is obvious. Thank you, I have no further questions.''

''Redirect?'' Heckemeyer asked.

''Sergeant Briscoe,'' Claire began, ''did you find the answering machine?''

''Yes, sir, we did.''

''And was there a new tape in it?''

''No, sir, there was not.''

''Then a reasonable person might assume

that he was trying to get rid of the tape, rather than merely replace it. Isn't that so?"

"Objection, calls for conclusion."

"Withdraw the question. Thank you, Sergeant. No further questions."

"Your Honor, the State calls Dr. Herb Ahlvin to the stand."

Dr. Ahlvin was the pathologist. He was sworn in, then took his seat for the questioning.

"Dr. Ahlvin, you examined the body of Dr. Gary Shaw, the decedent?"

"I did."

"And what was the cause of death?"

"The cause of death was an intrusive defect just above and to the left of the right ventricle. It was caused by the introduction of—"

Stone held up his hands. "In layman's terms, Doctor, please."

"The cause of death was a gunshot wound to the heart."

"Was the bullet still in the body when you examined it?"

"Yes."

Stone walked over to the evidence table and picked up a small plastic bag. "I show you this bullet and ask if it is the bullet you removed from Dr. Shaw's heart?"

"That is my signature on the chain-of-evidence card," Ahlvin said, looking at the bullet and the little tag.

"Thank you, Doctor. Your witness, counselor."

"Dr. Ahlvin," Moore began. "Would you say death was instantaneous?"

"Medically speaking, yes."

"Are you aware that a piece of paper was found next to the body, with the letters T-A?"

"Yes."

"The handwriting experts are divided as to whether or not Dr. Shaw wrote those two letters. Do you think he did?"

"I have no way of knowing."

"You did say death was instantaneous, didn't you?"

"I said, medically speaking, it was instantaneous."

"Well, what does that mean?"

"Within a few seconds."

"How few?"

"I have no way of knowing."

"Let me rephrase the question. Given the nature of the wound, could you say he died within less than five seconds?"

"Yes."

"It would be pretty difficult, wouldn't it, for someone with that kind of trauma to begin to write a note?"

"I would say yes."

"You are an expert witness, Doctor, and therefore your opinion is valid. In your opinion, did Dr. Shaw, with a wound such as he sustained, write that note?''

"In my opinion, he did not."

"Thank you, Dr. Ahlvin. No further questions."

Stone stood up. "Dr. Ahlvin, suppose Dr. Shaw was in the midst of writing the note before he was shot. Do you believe the wound could have stopped him in his tracks, so to speak? In other words, could he have gotten as far as T-A and then suffer a trauma severe enough to prevent him from doing as much as one more letter?''

"Yes, that is possible."

"Thank you, Doctor."

After Dr. Ahlvin, there were witnesses from the police lab. The most important witness was the fingerprint expert.

"We have several good, clear prints, yes," Mr. Adams answered Stone's question.

"Have you matched them all?''

"We have."

"Who do they belong to?''

"In the outer office we have fingerprints from Miss Judy Singleton, the receptionist. We also have fingerprints from Dr. David Corrigan, Dr. Linda Kasabian, and Dr. Gary Shaw. In addition, we have fingerprints from three more employees and the two men of Busy Bee Cleaning Service. We have two sets of prints that do not belong to employees or staff members. We have prints from Jerry Talbot and from Paul Alfusco.

"In Dr. Shaw's office, we found the expected prints from the staff members, plus a set of prints from Paul Alfusco."

"Where did you find Mr. Alfusco's prints?" Stone asked.

"We found them on the front of the desk. They were from his left hand, as if he had leaned forward."

"Did you find any prints on any of the computers, other than those you would normally expect to be there?"

"No, we did not."

"Thank you. Your witness."

Moore looked up from his table. "No questions."

"How many more witnesses do you have, Mr. Stone?" Judge Heckemeyer asked.

"Quite a few, Your Honor."

"Then let's save them until tomorrow, shall we? Court is recessed."

"How do you think we did?" Claire asked anxiously.

"There's no score," Stone said. "It's still anyone's ball game."

Chapter Nine

Mama Santangelo's restaurant

"**H**ave some more cheese," Mike Logan said, passing the plate across the table. "Uhm, no thank you," Stone replied, holding his hand out to decline.

"You don't like it?" Logan asked.

"No, I do like it. I like it too well, that's the problem. You forget, I'm not as active as you are. I don't have the opportunity to work it off."

"Have some more peppers," Briscoe said. "They aren't fattening."

"I'm afraid the peppers don't agree with me."

"I'll have some more," Claire said, taking a

181

few. She picked one up by the stem and bit it off, taking the whole pepper in her mouth.

"It must be nice to be young and have a stomach of cast iron," Stone said.

"Don't go pulling the Methuselah bit on me," Claire said. "You're old, but you aren't exactly dottering."

Briscoe laughed. "Would you call that a back-handed compliment?"

"And after I told her how well she did with her opening statement today," Stone said.

Logan carved off another piece of cheese. "Listen," he said. "How do you feel about this case?"

"What do you mean?" Stone replied.

"I mean, are you comfortable with it?" Logan asked.

Stone took a drink of wine, then patted his lips with a napkin before he answered. "Why do you ask that now, Mike? Are you having second thoughts about the case?"

"Not exactly second thoughts," Logan answered. "But I'm beginning to wish we had taken a little longer time with the first thought."

"What's wrong?" Claire asked. "Has something new turned up?"

Logan drummed his fingers on the table for a moment.

"Did you know that Kasabian and Corrigan were sleeping together?"

"Were sleeping together? Or, *are* sleeping together?" Stone asked.

"Were."

"Damn," Stone said. "I wish I had known that."

"I'm sorry. We just found out about it," Briscoe said.

"You're sure of it?"

"We're sure. There's a small country inn upstate where they've spent several weekends together."

"So now we're left with the question . . . is there some ulterior motive for Dr. Kasabian coming to us with the information?" Logan asked.

"You mean a woman scorned?" Claire asked.

"Something like that, yeah," Logan replied.

"That's a pretty chauvinistic attitude, isn't it? I mean, what makes you think she was scorned in the first place? Maybe she was the one who ended the affair."

"Don't get so defensive about it, Miss Kincaid," Briscoe said. "We don't mean this as anti-women or anything. But let's face it. If we're thinking about this, then you better believe Moore is."

"If he knows about it," Claire said.

"How can he help but know? Corrigan is going to tell him," Briscoe said.

"Yes, that's right. I suppose he would, wouldn't he? That would be a typical male response."

"Listen, if we can get over this battle of the sexes, we need to think about this," Stone said. "I believe you're right, Mike. Moore probably is going to use the tactic of a woman scorned striking back in any way she can to hurt Corrigan. So we're going to have to accommodate ourselves to that."

"Do you think there's any chance that it might be true?" Claire asked.

Stone picked up a large, black olive. "What you're really asking, Claire, is two questions. Question number one is, did Corrigan really do it? And question number two is, was Dr. Kasabian motivated by rejection to testify against him?"

"Well?"

Stone ate the olive, chewing it thoughtfully before he answered. Then he shook his head.

"If the answer to question number one is yes, Corrigan *did* commit the murder, then question number two is moot. Because it really doesn't matter why Kasabian came to us with the evidence, only that the evidence is accurate."

"All right, then that leaves the one big question. Did Corrigan really do it? Or have we been led down the primrose path?"

"You want my gut instinct?" Briscoe asked.

"Yeah," Stone said. "It won't count for anything in a court of law, but it has weight with me. What is your gut instinct?"

"My gut instinct is that Corrigan is guilty as hell."

"Mike?"

Logan lay his finger alongside his nose for a moment. "Yeah," he finally said, nodding in the affirmative. "Corrigan is guilty all right. But there's a smell to this. You two watch your ass. I've got a feeling that something's about to explode right in our face."

New York Superior Court, next day

"Please state your name."

"My name is Jeremiah Edward Talbot."

"Raise your right hand please. Do you swear to tell the truth, the whole truth, and nothing but the truth, so help you God?"

"I do."

"You may be seated."

Talbot sat down, then brushed his hand through his hair as Claire approached him.

"Are you employed, Mr. Talbot?" Claire asked.

"Yes."

"And what is your occupation?"

"I am director of the ACLW."

"That is a paid position?"

"Yes."

"What exactly is ACLW?"

"ACLW stands for Action Committee for Life Watch. The ACLW opposes the abortion advocates."

"I see. Now, Mr. Talbot, have you targeted Humaricare for your demonstrations?"

"Yes."

"You have had demonstrators there for how long?"

"Ever since we heard they were developing an abortion pill that would make baby killing even easier than the RU 486."

"The RU 486. That's the abortion pill developed in France?"

"Yes. Ironic, isn't it?"

Claire looked confused. "Ironic?"

"I mean how something so evil could have such an innocuous sounding name. RU 486. Zyklon B."

"Zyklon B?"

"That was the agent used by the Nazis in the gas chambers of their death camps," Talbot said.

"Objection!" Moore, the defense counsel, shouted. "The business about Zyklon B is irrelevant, Your Honor."

"Sustained. Mr. Talbot, you'll not use the witness stand to proselytize your point of view."

"Sorry, Your Honor. I was just answering a question."

"Miss Kincaid, you will keep your questions more narrowly focused."

"Yes, Your Honor," Claire said. "Mr. Talbot, on the night of August eleventh, did you visit the Humaricare clinic?"

"I did."

"And did you make an unlawful entry into the building?"

"Yes."

"What was the purpose of that unlawful entry?"

"I wanted to leave a poster of protest."

"That was the same poster described by Officer Milsap yesterday?"

"Yes."

"How did you get into the building?"

"Through the door."

"Did you force the door?"

"No. It was open."

"Open? Do you mean it was standing open?"

"It was unlocked."

"So you just opened it and walked in?"

"Yes."

"Did you see anything inside out of the ordinary?"

"No."

"No file cabinets opened, no paper scattered on the floor?"

"No."

"What about the computers? Did you see any computers?"

"I saw one on the desk there in front."

"Was it on or off?"

"I think it was off. I didn't pay any particular attention to it."

"But you believe it was off?"

"The screen was dark."

"Do you know if anyone else was on the premises at that time?"

"Yes."

"Who else was there?"

"Dr. Shaw."

"Did you see him?"

"Yes."

"Did he see you?"

"No."

"Tell the court the circumstances under which you saw him."

"I heard someone down the hall. I sneaked down the hall to see who it was and what was going on, and there I saw Dr. Shaw, sitting at his desk, talking on the phone."

"Do you know who he was talking to? Did you hear him say a name?"

"No."

"Did you hear anything that you could understand?"

"Yes."

"What did you hear?"

"I heard him say, 'You know damn well what's wrong. We need to talk and we need to talk now.'"

"Do you have any idea what that referred to?"

"No."

"What did you do then?"

"I didn't do anything. I had already pinned the poster to the back wall, so I left."

"That's all?"

"Yes."

"Did you go into any of the other offices?"

"No. Just the reception area, the hallway, and Dr. Shaw's office. Actually, I didn't even go into his office, I just looked inside."

"Did you look through Dr. Corrigan's desk?"

"No, I did not."

"Did you find Dr. Corrigan's gun?"

"No, I did not."

"Did you take the gun down the hallway into Dr. Shaw's office?"

"No, I did not."

"Did you shoot Dr. Shaw?"

"No, I did not."

"How long were you inside the clinic?"

"From the time I stepped through until the time I left couldn't have been more than a minute, or a minute and a half."

"When you left, how did you leave?"

"The same way I came in. I left by the front door."

"Did you lock the door when you left?"

"No. Well, actually, I couldn't have locked it even if I had wanted to. You need the keys to lock it."

"I see. Where did you go after you left?"

"I went back to my apartment."

"When you returned to your apartment that night, did you talk to anyone?"

"I didn't see anyone. I did make a telephone call."

"Who did you talk to?"

"I called Paul Alfusco and told him what I had done."

"Why did you feel it was necessary to tell Mr. Alfusco?"

"Paul Alfusco's a pro in this, you know? I mean he was protesting back in the sixties when I was just a kid. I remember reading about him —how he poured blood on his draft card, how he marched in front of an American Legion parade, carrying the V.C. flag. How he lay down on the tracks in front of troop trains. He really put himself on the line for what he believed in then. I respected him for that, and I wanted him to know that I was willing to take risks too."

"I see. Thank you, Mr. Talbot. I have no further questions."

Moore stood up and walked over to stand halfway between the witness chair and the jury.

"Mr. Talbot, what do you think about the work Dr. Corrigan is doing?"

"Objection, Your Honor!" Stone shouted quickly. "Defense counsel protested vigorously when he thought our line of questioning was getting off the path, and now he is trying to bring up the very thing he protested."

"Your Honor, Jerry Talbot is a witness for the prosecution," Moore said. "He is also a well-known anti-abortion activist. I think it is important for the jury to know just how Mr. Talbot feels, personally, about the nature of Dr. Corrigan's work. I believe when the jury sees how passionately this man is committed to his own agenda, they will realize that he may have a vested interest in giving testimony that will be detrimental to my client."

"Your Honor, he can't have his cake and eat it too," Stone insisted.

Judge Heckemeyer rapped his gavel once. "Court will take a ten-minute recess. Counselors, see me in my chambers."

Once inside the judge's chambers, Judge

Heckemeyer lit a cigarette. He exhaled with a long, satisfied sigh.

"It was almost worth having you get into it just to give me an opportunity to have a cigarette," he said. He sat down and leaned back in his chair with the cigarette hanging from his mouth. "Now, what is all this, Mr. Moore? You made such a thing about eliminating all reference to abortion, and now here you are, wanting to bring it up."

"Judge, you know and I know, and Mr. Stone and Miss Kincaid know as well, that we can't just close our eyes to that issue. That's hanging over the courtroom like something palpable. Why do you think this case has garnered so much attention in the media? It is because of what it's about, that's why. When you get right down to it, no matter who killed Dr. Shaw, the motive was related to the abortion pill Humaricare is trying to develop. If we can't avoid it, then we may as well face it."

"Your Honor, he can't have it both ways," Stone said. "He can't object when we bring it up, then go right back to it himself."

"Actually I objected to the reference to Zyklon B in the same vein as an abortion pill. And if you're truthful about it, Stone, you'll admit that you don't particularly want that reference either."

"I'll grant you that," Stone said.

Judge Heckemeyer butted his cigarette in a brass ashtray, then stood up.

"I'm going to let you fish in this stream a little longer, Mr. Moore," he said. "But I'm going to keep my eye on you. I'll not let my courtroom be turned into a soapbox."

"Thank you, Your Honor," Moore said.

"Do you have a problem with that, Mr. Stone?"

"No, Your Honor. As long as I know the rules, I can play the game."

"Let's get back out there."

Three sharp raps of the gavel brought the courtroom back to order.

"You may continue with your questioning, Mr. Moore," Judge Heckemeyer said.

"May I have the last question read back to me?" Moore asked.

" 'Tell me, Mr. Talbot, what do you think of the work Dr. Corrigan is doing?' " the clerk read. The clerk then added, "The question is under objection."

"Thank you," Moore said. He looked at the judge. "Your Honor?"

"Objection overruled. Witness may answer the question."

"I hate what he's doing," Talbot said. "Do you realize there were thirty-eight million abortions, worldwide, last year? Thirty-eight million!

That is equivalent to killing every man, woman, and child in Australia and Canada combined. Think what an uproar that would cause. And if the abortion pills, the RU 486 and the PEBC, come into general use, it could quadruple the number of abortions in one year. That would equal Australia, Canada, England, and France. Not even Hitler was that successful.''

''What would you do to stop the development of this pill?''

''Whatever I have to do.''

''Thank you, Mr. Talbot. I have no further questions.''

''No redirect, Your Honor,'' Stone said.

''Ben, you're going to let that stand?'' Claire hissed.

''Moore wants us to argue the ethics and morality of abortion. That would reinforce his suggestion that Corrigan is the victim, rather than the guilty party. We're going to get enough of this with our next witness. Go ahead and call him.''

Claire nodded, then stood up. ''Your Honor, the State calls Paul Antony Alfusco.''

There were many in the gallery who could remember the name Alfusco from the sixties, and they stretched and strained to get a look at this icon from the turbulent past.

''Mr. Alfusco, what is your employment?''

''I'm a free-lance writer, articles, short stories,

books. I wrote the book *Bombs and Barricades,* about the protest movement in the sixties."

"You were an active protester in the sixties?"

"Yes."

"And now you are active with the ACLW?"

"Yes."

"In that role, were you at the Humaricare clinic on August eleventh?" Claire asked.

"Yes, I was."

"What time were you there?"

"I was there from eight in the morning until five that afternoon, demonstrating against what was going on inside the clinic."

"Are you part of a group called Wednesday's Children?"

"I beg your pardon?" Moore asked from his seat behind the defense table.

"Wednesday's Children," Claire said again, more slowly this time.

"Yes. That's what the protesters who are there on Wednesday call themselves."

"As I understand it, you are divided into 'day teams,' and each team has a day in which they're present to protest. Is that right?"

"Yes."

"Mr. Alfusco, your day is Wednesday. But you were there the next morning, were you not? You were seen there on Thursday morning, just after eight o'clock."

"Yes. I was there the next morning."

"Why?"

"I knew Dr. Shaw had been shot, so I came down to see what was going to happen."

"How did you know Dr. Shaw had been shot? No information had been released yet."

"I knew he had been shot because I saw his body during the night, before the police discovered it."

There was a collective gasp from many in the gallery.

"You were inside the Humaricare building during the night?"

"Yes."

"Why were you there, Mr. Alfusco?"

"Jerry Talbot called me at around eleven or eleven-thirty. I'm not sure of the exact time. What he told me got me to thinking, and the more I thought about it, the more worried I got."

"What did he tell you when he called?"

"He said, 'I just put my ass on the line. I've been inside the clinic.' "

"Why did you worry about that?"

"Earlier in the day we'd been talking about the shooting down in Florida, and out in Kansas. I told him that although I didn't approve of what they did, I could remember the passion from the anti-war protest days and I knew what it was like to put your ass on the line. When he used that same term with me . . . I wasn't sure what he had done. So, I decided to go down to the clinic myself and have a look around."

"What happened when you got there?"

"The front door was locked."

"The front door was locked?"

"Yes."

"Are you sure about that?"

"Yes, I'm positive."

"You heard Mr. Talbot testify here earlier that the door was unlocked for him, didn't you?"

"Yes."

"And you heard him say that he did not lock the door when he left?"

"I heard what he said, but I'm telling you, the front door was locked."

"What did you do then?"

"I found a loose brick and tossed it through the front window. Then I stepped through to go inside."

"What did you see?"

"I saw the poster that Jerry told me about. I also saw that the computer was on."

"How do you know the computer was on?"

"There was something running across the screen. You know, like one of those screen saver programs?"

"What did you do then?"

"I walked through all the offices, just to take a look around. That's when I found him."

"Dr. Shaw?"

"Yes."

"Could you describe the scene?"

"It was just exactly the way the policeman described it yesterday," Alfusco said. "Dr. Shaw was slumped across his desk, dead."

"What did you do?"

"I stood there for a moment, sort of dumbstruck. Then I saw the empty shell casing on the floor in front of the desk, so I picked it up and dropped it in my pocket."

"That seems like a curious thing to do."

"I know. I guess I wasn't thinking all that clearly. I was certain that Jerry had killed him, and the only thing I could think of was that the empty shell casing might be a clue that could connect him to the murder. So I figured if I picked it up, it would keep the police from finding out who did it."

"Did you scatter the files?"

"Yes. I thought it might further confuse the issue."

"Mr. Alfusco, the police have been unable to find the murder weapon. Did you, by any chance, pick it up?"

"No. Just the empty casing."

"After you picked up the empty casing and scattered the papers about, what did you do?"

"I left. I thought about going by Jerry's place to give him hell for what he had done . . . or at least, what I thought he had done. Then I decided that it might not look good if we were seen together that night. So I just went back home."

"How did you leave?"

"I beg your pardon?"

"How did you leave the building? Did you go through the door?"

"No, I told you, the door was locked. I went back out the same way I came in. Through the broken window."

"Thank you, Mr. Alfusco. I have no further questions. Your witness, Mr. Moore."

"Thank you," Moore said. "Mr. Alfusco, you said you made your living as a freelance writer?"

"Yes."

"How do you write?"

"I beg your pardon?"

"I've always been fascinated by how writers write. Some write with a pencil, some with a typewriter. I once read that Hemingway stood up to type his stories. How do you write?"

"Nothing so dramatic, I'm afraid. I use a computer."

"A computer?"

"Yes."

"So you are what they call computer literate, then? Yes, of course you are. You recognized the screen saver on the computer in the Humaricare building. On the night of the eleventh of August, did you tell anyone you were going down to the Humaricare Clinic?''

"Tell anyone? No, who would I have told?''

"Talbot, perhaps?''

"No, I didn't tell him.''

"No, you didn't tell him, because you didn't want him to know that you were going down there, did you?''

"No.''

"Because he had just provided you with the perfect cover, hadn't he?''

"Perfect cover? I don't know what you're getting at.''

"Didn't you just testify that Talbot called you, and told you he had broken into the Humaricare building?''

"Yes.''

"So you figured you could go down there as well and, no matter what you did, the blame would be placed on Talbot.''

"I don't know what you are getting at.''

"Well, it's quite simple, Mr. Alfusco. You had a free shot, didn't you?''

"I didn't look at it that way.''

"Didn't you? Mr. Alfusco, does the name Benny Brewster mean anything to you?''

"Who?''

"Ben, what's he talking about?'' Claire whispered.

"I don't know," Stone answered, leaning forward to pay particular attention to the direction the cross-examination was going.

"Benny Brewster. You do remember him, don't you, Mr. Alfusco?"

"I'm not sure."

"I have located Benny Brewster, Mr. Alfusco. He is working for the New York Port Authority. I could have him here in less than an hour. I'm sure he remembers you quite well. Should I get him?"

"No," Alfusco said. "That won't be necessary. I remember him now."

"Your Honor, approach the bench?" Stone called.

"Very well, you may approach."

Stone and Claire approached the bench to join Moore, who was already there.

"Your Honor, I'd like to know where all this is going?" Stone said.

"I'd like to know as well," the judge said.

"Mr. Alfusco has a history of following break-ins," Moore said. "In 1968 a man named Benny Brewster broke into an ROTC building. He splashed paint around, tore up some furniture, and trashed the place, but that was all. Alfusco went into the same building later and planted a bomb. Fortunately, the bomb didn't hurt anyone, but it did do a lot of damage, more damage than Brewster's vandalism. The bottom line is, Alfusco copped a plea. Suspended sentence for what he did, in return for his testimony against Brewster. The government was beginning to crack down hard on war protesters then, so they came down hard on Brewster. He got five years."

"How is that relevant to this case?" Stone asked.

"Don't you see? It's the same pattern. Alfusco follows Talbot in a break-in."

"You may proceed, Mr. Alfusco," Heckemeyer said.

"Thank you, Your Honor."

Stone and Claire retook their seats.

"Mr. Alfusco, you have had a moment or two to recall. Do you remember Bennie Brewster now?"

"Yes."

"Did you know him in 1968?"

"Yes."

"How did you know him?"

"We participated in some anti-war demonstrations."

"Did one of those demonstrations involve Kensington College? I refer particularly to the incident with the ROTC building at Kensington. Did you demonstrate against the ROTC at Kensington?"

Alfusco sighed. "Yes."

"As I recall, Mr. Brewster broke into the building then and vandalized it. Is that right?"

"Yes."

"And afterward, taking advantage of the fact that someone else had already broken in, you went in as well, didn't you? You figured you could do anything you wanted and get away with it, because Brewster had already broken in."

"It wasn't exactly like that," Alfusco said.

"But you did go in afterward, didn't you?"

"Yes, but—"

"No qualifications are needed, Mr. Alfusco. You either did or you didn't. And it is a matter of public record that you did, because you planted a bomb in the building, didn't you?"

"Yes," Alfusco said, speaking the word so quietly that it could barely be heard.

"What did you say?" Moore asked, cupping his hand behind his ear. "You'll have to speak up. I didn't hear you."

"I said yes, I did plant a bomb. But no one was hurt."

"No one was hurt, that is true. But the building was so badly damaged that it was a year before classes could be held there again. Am I right?"

Alfusco grinned broadly. "ROTC classes never returned," he said. "The school dropped the program."

"Do you consider that the result of your activity there?"

"I know it is the result of my activity there."

"So, in your mind, the end justified the means?"

"We got out of Vietnam. People aren't dying there anymore. Yes, I think the end justified the means."

"If you feel that, why didn't you have the courage to accept the responsibility for what you did?"

"I did accept the responsibility for what I did. I confessed to being the one who planted the bomb."

"Yes, as part of a plea bargain. Isn't it true, Mr. Alfusco, that you testified against Benny Brewster in exchange for a suspended sentence? And isn't it true that Benny Brewster, for spreading a little paint around, received a five-year prison sentence, while you received a suspended sentence for planting a bomb?"

"Those were difficult, more turbulent times. There was a bigger question involved than the mere breaking and entering of an ROTC building."

"Just as there is a bigger question involved now, than breaking and entering the Humaricare clinic?"

"There is a bigger question, yes, but it isn't the same thing."

"Oh? I think it is, Mr. Alfusco. I think it was déjà vu for you. I think you saw an opportunity to repeat your great victory of 1968. You stopped the ROTC program and you were going to stop the development of the PEBC project. Isn't that the way it was?"

"No. I've already testified that something Talbot said made me nervous."

"Yes, I recall. But you know what I think, Mr. Alfusco? I think you went down there to enlarge upon what Talbot did. I think you went down there to scatter the files and purge the computers. By your own admission, you are computer literate; it would be fairly easy to introduce a virus if you already had one on a disk."

"That's not true. I didn't touch the computers."

"Oh, I think it is true. And you know what else I think is true? I think you found Dr. Corrigan's pistol. Then I think you went down to Dr. Shaw's office, intending to go through his desk as well. But Dr. Shaw was working late that night . . . so involved in his work that he didn't hear the glass front break. I think you surprised him . . . and he surprised you. And I think you shot him. Then you picked up the empty shell casing, intending to get rid of it, and the gun. The gun, you got rid of somewhere. After all, it's a major clue. But the shell casing is small, and you forgot about it. You forgot about it and you went home, secure in the feeling that Talbot would be blamed for the murder instead of you. But the police found the empty shell casing, didn't they? They found it in your apartment, and you thought you were going to get blamed after all. What a pleasant surprise it must've been when Dr. Corrigan was accused instead of you."

"That's not true. I didn't kill Dr. Shaw," Alfusco said agitatedly.

"You didn't?"

"No, I did not," Alfusco said resolutely.

"Well, I wouldn't worry about it if I were you. After all, you don't have to convince me. I'm neither the judge nor the jury. I'm just the defense counsel for a man who is wrongly accused, that's all. I have no further questions, Your Honor."

Stone stood up. "Mr. Alfusco, did you purge the computers?"

"No, sir, I did not."

"Did you shoot Dr. Shaw?"

"No, sir, I did not."

"No further questions."

"Witness is excused," Judge Heckemeyer said. He cleared his throat and looked over at the counselors for both sides.

"I have a series of meetings tomorrow which

I cannot put off. Therefore, unless one of you has a compelling reason why we cannot suspend the proceedings for one day, we will reconvene at nine o'clock, day after tomorrow.''

Chapter Ten

HRH Dumplin's, a restaurant on 52nd Street

The waiter, a thin, blond-haired man in his late thirties to mid-forties, removed his glasses and polished them, then put them back on and, without being seen, studied the man and woman he had just seated at the corner table. The table was the darkest and most poorly illuminated in the entire restaurant, and as soon as they were seated, the man further darkened it by snuffing out the candle that had previously lighted the distance between them.

Ordinarily Bruce Parkinson wouldn't be so interested in his customers . . . especially if, by their action, they made it known that they wanted their privacy. But this was not an ordinary circumstance. Unless he was terribly mistaken, he had just been reading about the man and woman who were now sitting at the corner table.

He'd been reading the *Post,* with its glaring headlines and oversized pictures of all the principals of what the media were now calling the Abortion Pill Murder trial. For a moment he couldn't recall where he had left it, then remembered and went into the cloakroom to check it out.

"Bruce, you have customers at their tables," the maitre d' told him when he saw Bruce looking through the paper. "I do hope whatever you're reading is interesting."

"I'll be right with them," Bruce replied. "There's something I've got to . . . yes. Yes, here it is. Damn, it *is* them."

"Who is them?"

"That couple at table eighteen," Bruce said. "Do you know who they are? I never thought I would see them together."

"Don't tell me. It's Burt and Loni."

"No. It's the people from that trial."

"What trial?"

"Haven't you been watching the news?"

"I don't watch anything but my daytime soaps," the maitre d' said.

"Well, if you had been, you would know who I'm talking about. There's a big murder trial going on right now, and Dr. Corrigan, the guy that they think is the murderer, is here."

"Here? In Dumplin's?"

"At table eighteen."

"Are you sure?"

"Yes, I'm sure. That's why I came to check the paper."

"What's he doing out of jail? Do you think maybe he's escaped or something? Maybe we should call the police."

"No, he hasn't escaped or anything. I'm sure he's out on bail. I mean he's a rich and famous doctor, he wouldn't have any problem making bail. But it is sort of strange seeing him here with her."

"Who her?"

"Dr. Kasabian. According to all the stories, she's going to testify for the prosecution. So if she's going to testify against him . . . what are they doing together?"

Claire Kincaid's apartment, the same evening

Settling down with a salad and a cup of hot tea, Claire turned television on to the Brook Lee show, *Spectrum*. Now, and for the duration of the trial, his show was dedicated entirely to the trial. Claire wished she was blasé enough to disregard the show. In fact, Ben had told her it would better if she didn't watch, but she couldn't help herself. She supposed it was a little like a Broadway actress reading her reviews.

"Good evening, ladies and gentlemen. I'm Brook Lee and you are watching Spectrum. *Thank you for tuning in. My guests tonight, as they have been every night since the 'Abortion Pill Murder' trial began, are Mason Alexander and Dexter Keene. Mason Alexander is our spokesperson,"* Lee came down hard on the word person, *"representing the pro-choice people, while Dexter Keene is the spokesman for the pro-life people. Let me say that the emphasis on spokesperson and spokesman is in keeping with their wishes, and we have also settled upon the use of the terms pro-choice and pro-life.*

"Now, having gotten through all that, let's begin our discussion. Mr. Alexander, I believe you have the opening word tonight. How did you think things went today?"

"As you no doubt noticed, Brook, all the earlier witnesses, the perfunctory type witnesses that you would have in any murder case, gave their testimony in a professional, and nonprejudicial manner. We heard the policemen, and the medical examiner, and the lab people present their evidence. Today, however, the true colors began to show and things turned nasty when the prosecution introduced Jerry Talbot and Paul Alfusco."

"Turned nasty?" Brook asked.

"Yes. You saw it. The prosecutor, Ms. Kincaid, allowing Talbot to make that ridiculous comparison between abortion and the holocaust."

"Hold on there, fella!" Claire said, speaking to the TV. "I didn't bring that up, and I wasn't expecting it."

"Wait a minute, wait a minute!" Dexter Keene said on the screen. *"What do you mean a ridiculous comparison? I thought Mr. Talbot made the point quite clearly. Thirty-eight million babies killed every year!"*

"Now that's exactly what I'm talking about!" Alexander said. *"Even if those numbers were true—and I'm not accepting for one moment that they are—they don't mean anything. You aren't killing babies, you are preventing a birth. I mean if you were going to use that kind of logic, you could probably decide how many times birth control devices are used, from condoms to the pill to the totally discredited rhythm method, and come up with an even more amazing number."*

"Are you equating birth control with abortion?" Keene asked.

"No, I'm not equating birth control with abortion. I'm just going to an extreme to make a point."

"It is interesting though, isn't it?" Keene replied. *"I mean how quickly and easily the comparison came to mind. How you were able to think of birth control and abortion as if the two were the same."*

"*Let's be fair, Mr. Keene. I don't think he was saying there was no difference between birth control and abortion,*" Brook Lee said.

"*Oh, but he was,*" Keene insisted. "*And that's exactly what I and people like me have been trying to point out all along. Don't you see? If you make abortion as simple as birth control, then before you know it, there won't be any difference at all. Good Lord, man, they're already passing out condoms in grade schools. In grade schools, mind you. I don't think it's too farfetched to imagine school nurses of the future passing out abortion pills along with aspirins and Band-Aids.*"

"*That is exactly the kind of hyperbole that is preventing us from having any kind of rational discussion of this issue,*" Alexander insisted. "*You know that isn't going to happen but you are suggesting that it might, as a sort of scare tactic.*"

"*I don't think it's going to happen? Let me tell you something. If you had asked me twenty years ago—ten years ago even—if I thought the schools would ever be passing out condoms to children, I would have said of course not. When I was a kid you had to buy them from machines on the walls in service station men's rooms. Now they're school supplies, right alongside notebook paper, number-two pencils, and crayons. Do you really think abortion pills won't become school issue within another decade or so?*"

"*Please, gentlemen, please,*" Lee said, holding up his hands to interrupt the bickering. "*Let's* not lose sight of the issue of our program. We are supposed to be discussing the trial of Dr. David Corrigan. How has it gone, and where does it go from here? Bottom line please, Mr. Alexander. And Mr. Keene, if you would, please allow him to finish."

"Bottom line? I think prosecution hurt their case by putting Talbot and Alfusco on the witness stands today," Alexander said. "They were so full of their own agenda that they added nothing to the indictment against Dr. Corrigan."

"What about Defense's ploy in suggesting that, perhaps, Alfusco himself might be guilty?" Lee asked.

"You called it like it is," Keene said. "It was nothing but a ploy, and I don't think the jury will buy it for one minute."

"I agree with Mr. Keene in that I don't believe the jury will accept the idea that Alfusco is the guilty party and is just, somehow, hanging around in the wings watching someone else squirm in his place. But I do think that the defense scored some points by suggesting that he was."

"How is that, if you don't think the jury will buy into it?" Lee asked.

"It's just as Thurman Moore said. He isn't a prosecutor, and he doesn't have to convince the jury that Paul Alfusco is guilty. All he has to do is convince the jury that it is not entirely impossible that Alfusco might be guilty. And if his tactic leaves some doubt in the jury's mind as to whether or not Alfusco could be guilty, then that means there is also a doubt as to *whether or not Dr. Corrigan is guilty. And a little doubt is all that is needed. Remember, to succeed, Prosecution has to convince the jury, beyond a reasonable doubt, that Dr. Corrigan is guilty."*

"The judge gave them a one-day break, so the trial won't begin again until day after tomorrow," Lee said. "What do you see happening then?"

"Day after tomorrow should tell the tale," Alexander replied. "Prosecution will be going with their star witness."

"You are talking about Dr. Linda Kasabian."

"Yes. Dr. Kasabian has been involved in the research from the beginning. She knows all the twists and turns and the secrets. And if, as the prosecution claims, this is really no more than a dispute over how much progress they have actually made, then she should be able to shed light on it."

"I agree," Keene said. "Kasabian is the key to the whole thing."

"What do you think? Does she have the goods? And, more importantly, will she be able to deliver?" Lee asked.

"Oh, I think she has the goods all right," Lee said. "If she didn't, the case would've never gone to court."

"Do you think prosecution is taking a chance?" Lee asked.

"Not really. I'm sure that they have all the bases covered. I think what we have seen up until now has just been so much fluff. The real trial starts day after tomorrow."

"What about you, Mr. Keene? Do you go along with that?"

"Only partially," Keene said. *"I agree that prosecution's case against Dr. Corrigan won't really start until day after tomorrow. But from the very beginning this has been a case of much larger proportions than the possible murder of one abortionist by another."*

"Oh no, here we go again," Alexander said. *"Abortionists? They're not abortionists, for God's sake. They are research doctors! And the trial is no larger than the incident of murder . . . which is actually large enough if you stop and consider it."*

"No, it's much larger than a simple murder, and if you'll listen to me for a moment, I can convince you that I am right," Keene insisted.

"All right, as Ross Perot says, I'm all ears," Alexander said.

Brook Lee laughed appreciatively.

"Do you know how many murder cases are being tried in this city right now?" Keene asked.

"No, I'm afraid not."

"Twelve. There are twelve cases in court as of this very moment. Can you name the others? In fact, can you name even one of the others?"

"No, but what does that have to do with what we're talking about?"

"It has everything to do with what we're talking about," Keene insisted. *"We're here to discuss this case because of who we are and what it is. You represent the pro-abor—excuse me, I promised that for dis-*

219

cussion purposes I wouldn't refer to you that way. You represent the pro-choice people, and I represent the pro-life people. We are highly visible members of our representative groups. And the case we're discussing deals not just with a simple murder, but with people who are involved in research to come up with an abortion pill. This case is being followed by the entire nation. Do you think for one minute there would be this much interest in it if Corrigan and Shaw were bakers who had a falling out over how much sugar to put on a doughnut?"

"No, I'll grant you that. But I don't see what that has to do with anything."

"You said that everything up until now was fluff and that the real trial won't start until day after tomorrow. And I say that the real trial is, and has been, the national focus on the issue of abortion. And that trial started several days ago. If you are intellectually honest with yourself, Mr. Alexander, you will realize that it doesn't really matter whether Dr. Corrigan killed Dr. Shaw or not. That murder is of no real consequence to the national interest in this trial. And the verdict, be it guilty or not guilty, will be a complete anti-climax."

"And with that note, we have come to the end of today's show," Lee said. He looked into the camera. *"Dr. Kasabian testifies day after tomorrow. Tune in tomorrow night and we'll discuss what she's likely to say during her testimony. Until then, this is* Spectrum, *and I am Brook Lee. Good night."*

Claire turned the TV off feeling a sense of disquiet over the way the discussion had gone. Ben was right. She shouldn't have watched that trash.

Police station house, next morning

"Thanks for coming over, Ben," Briscoe said as Stone came into the police station. "We just got a rather interesting and unexpected slant on the Corrigan trial."

"What is it?"

"I think you'd better hear it for yourself," Briscoe suggested.

"I don't know if I want to hear it or not," Stone replied. He sighed. "But I suppose I have to. All right, where do I go now?"

"The person I want you to talk to is in Lieutenant Van Buren's office," Briscoe said. "Mike and the lieutenant are talking to him now."

"Who am I going to see?"

"Parkinson. Bruce Parkinson. He's a waiter at Dumplin's, which is a small, rather trendy restaurant in mid-Manhattan."

Stone followed Briscoe into the lieutenant's office. She was sitting behind her desk. Mike was standing up, leaning against a filing cabinet, while a third person, a thin, bespectacled blond-haired man was sitting primly on a chair with his legs crossed.

"Mr. Parkinson, I'm Benjamin Stone," Stone said as he came into the office.

"Yes, yes, I recognize you. I saw your picture on TV," Parkinson said.

"Sergeant Briscoe said you had some information for me."

"Yes. I don't know how important this is, but last night Dr. Corrigan and Dr. Kasabian had dinner together in my restaurant."

"Are you sure it was them?"

"Oh, absolutely."

"Do you know them? By that I mean, are they regular customers?" Stone asked.

Parkinson shook his head. "No, they aren't regulars," he said. "I don't think I've ever even seen them before, except for their pictures in the papers and on TV."

"What did they do?"

"They ordered dinner, then they just sat over in a dark corner of the restaurant. They didn't speak to anyone."

"This is too much to hope for, but, they didn't by any chance use a credit card, did they?"

"Yes, they did," Parkinson said. "And that's why I almost didn't come. I mean, I was certain as to who they were, from the moment they came in. Then when he paid with a credit card with a totally different name on it, I started thinking that perhaps I had made a mistake."

"You mean the card didn't have Corrigan or Kasabian's name?"

"No."

"What about Humaricare? Maybe it was a corporate card," Logan suggested.

"No, it was somebody's card. It belong to someone named Victor Trailins."

"That's it," Mike said, snapping his fingers and grinning broadly. "He's one of the lab technicians from Humaricare. There's all the connection we need."

"Sergeant Briscoe, I want you and Logan to pick up Dr. Kasabian," Lieutenant Van Buren said.

"Good idea," Stone agreed. "I think perhaps Dr. Kasabian and I need to have a little talk."

"Where do you want me to bring her? Here, or your office?"

Stone looked through the window of lieutenant Van Buren's office out across the bay area. It was a beehive of intimidating activity, with sullen suspects standing about in handcuffs. Stone smiled.

"Bring her here," he said. "It might make more of an impression."

"Let's go, partner," Briscoe said, starting for the door.

* * *

The receptionist frowned when she saw Briscoe and Logan.

"Good morning, Miss Singleton," Briscoe said.

"Is there something I can do for you?" she asked without enthusiasm.

"I don't know," Logan replied, smiling broadly. "I thought I might ask you out to the Policeman's Ball. I've got two tickets."

"Sorry, I'm busy," Judy said.

Logan snapped his fingers. "You know, now that I think about it, I am too," he said.

"If you are here to see Dr. Corrigan, he isn't here. He is on an indefinite leave of absence until after the trial."

"Until after the trial? You seem to be confident that he'll be back," Logan said.

"I am. I don't believe for one minute that he had anything to do with poor Dr. Shaw being killed."

"Actually, we're here to see Dr. Kasabian," Briscoe said.

"May I tell her you're here? Or would you rather break in her door?"

Logan chuckled. "You can tell her," he said.

Miss Singleton picked up the phone and touched a button. "Dr. Kasabian, those two men from the police department are here to see you." She hung up, then looked up at Briscoe and Logan. "She'll be right here."

Dr. Kasabian arrived a few moments later. "Yes?" she said. "What can I do for you?"

"Dr. Kasabian, I wonder if you could come down to the police station with us," Briscoe said. "We want to ask you a few questions."

"Oh . . . this isn't a good time," Dr. Kasabian replied. "Couldn't I come later?"

Logan shook his head. "Consider this one of those invitations you can't refuse," he said.

"All right," Dr. Kasabian answered. "I'll just get my purse."

"Miss Singleton will get it."

"What? What is this all about?"

"We would rather you stay here with us. Miss Singleton, would you get her purse, please?"

"All right," Miss Singleton said, obviously curious about what was going on.

"Thank you, Judy," Dr. Kasabian said. "You'll find it on the coat rack in my office."

The three waited in awkward silence in the reception area, until Miss Singleton returned with the purse. Then Logan held the front door open.

"Shall we go?" he invited.

Ben Stone was sitting at a table in one of the interrogation rooms when Briscoe and Logan brought Dr. Kasabian into the station.

"What is this room?" Dr. Kasabian asked.

"Why have you brought me down to this place?"

"This is where we interrogate suspects, Doctor," Stone said.

"I don't understand. Am I a suspect in something?"

"Let's just say you've behaved in a suspicious manner," Stone replied. "Dr. Kasabian, why did you have dinner with Corrigan last night?"

"Is that what this is all about? The fact that I had dinner with David last night?"

"Yes."

"Why would I be treated as a suspect, just because I had dinner with an old friend? And anyway, what business is it of yours? This is still a free country, isn't it? I can have dinner with anyone I please."

"Don't act so put upon, Doctor. You knew that would arouse our suspicion."

"No I didn't. Why should I know?"

"You did everything you could to avoid detection. You sat in a dark corner. You extinguished the candle. You paid for the meal with a credit card belonging to Victor Trailins. Why did you do all that if you didn't think what you were doing was suspect?"

"You had me followed, didn't you?" Dr. Kasabian said. "What right do you have to have me followed?"

"As a matter of fact, we didn't have you followed," Stone said. "A civic-minded citizen who has been following the trial in the newspapers thought it was a little unusual to see the prosecution's star witness cozying up to the defendant. Now if a disinterested citizen realizes that it's wrong for a prosecution witness to have a private dinner with the very defendant against whom she is going to testify, then surely you should as well. What is going on, Dr. Kasabian?"

Tears sprang to Dr. Kasabian's eyes. "You don't understand," she said.

"No, I don't. I would like you to enlighten me."

"David . . . that is, Dr. Corrigan and I were once very close."

"By very close, do you mean lovers?"

"Yes. But it all ended several months ago. Nothing either of us did, really. It was just that our careers—and the research—got in the way. It was very difficult to balance a love affair at night with difficult research decisions that had to be made during the day. We parted as friends."

"Go on," Stone said.

"David is very hurt to think that my testimony might convict him. He insists that he is innocent, and I want so much for him to be. We had the dinner last night at my suggestion. I wanted to tell him that I'm only going to tell the truth, and if he's innocent, the truth can only serve to free him. You must understand, I still care for him. I would not want to see him go to prison if he's innocent."

"And if he's not innocent?"

"If David is guilty . . . if he did kill Gary Shaw, then he's not the man I once loved. I wanted David to understand that as well. I'm sorry, Mr. Stone. You're right, I did know that it was wrong. We tried to keep our meeting last night a secret. That's why I borrowed Victor's credit card. I hope it hasn't upset everything."

"I hope it hasn't either," Stone said. He leaned back in the chair and studied Dr. Kasabian for a long moment. "All right, Doctor, you can go," he said. "But please, don't come up with any more surprises until this trial is over."

Dr. Kasabian smiled, then held up her hand. "I promise," she said. "I'll be as good as gold."

Stone drummed her fingers on the table for a long moment after Dr. Kasabian left.

"What do you think, Ben?" Logan asked.

"I think we have to suck it up and go on," he said. "At this point there's nothing else we can do. But I have to tell you—I feel as if we're up the proverbial creek without a paddle."

Chapter
Eleven

Superior Court

Dr. Linda Kasabian took her oath, then sat in the witness chair. Anyone following the case knew that the State was hanging their entire case upon her testimony, and every seat in the gallery was filled, many by reporters from newspapers across the country.

Ben Stone stood up to begin the questioning.

"Dr. Kasabian, could you give us a little of your background?"

"I graduated from the University of Chicago, attended medical school at Washington University in St. Louis. I have also studied at Tufts and Johns Hopkins. I spent three years at the Houston Medical Center before coming to Humaricare."

"Have you been published·in any of the medical journals?"

"Yes, several times. My most recent publication dealt with my research into progesterone"

"Progesterone?"

"It is a hormone produced by the ovaries, which allows the fertilized egg to develop."

"And that is relative to the research you have been doing?"

"Yes, very relative. If the fertilized egg does not receive progesterone, it cannot adhere to the inner lining of the uterine, thus development cannot occur."

"As much as you can, Dr. Kasabian, bearing in mind that you need to keep the explanation simple, could you explain the principle of the abortion pill?"

"The RU 486, which is the pill developed by Dr. Etienne-Emile Baulieu, works by blocking the progesterone . . . not letting it get through to the blastocyst. That has to be followed within a couple of days, either by an injection, or the ingestion, of prostaglandin, which will then cause the blastocyst to be expelled."

"The blastocyst?"

"The fertilized egg in its earliest stages. At this point it is not even an embryo, but merely a collection of cells."

"And how is the PEBC supposed to work?"

"Objection, Your Honor," Moore said. "The PEBC represents a major investment of time and money. To give the secrets away in court would be devastating to Humaricare and to all those who have invested in it."

"Your Honor, I will not ask Dr. Kasabian to disclose anything that has not previously been published. I am only asking for a layman's description of how the thing works."

"Objection overruled. The witness may tell, in broad, nonspecific terms, how the PEBC abortion pill is supposed to work."

"It is similar to the RU 486," Dr. Kasabian said, "in that it prevents progesterone from getting to the fertilized egg. The difference is, we intend to cause a temporary cessation of the progesterone production, rather than block it from the egg. In addition, the PEBC will neutralize the enzyme produced by the egg itself. That enzyme allows the egg to digest the surface cells and sink itself into the uterine lining. Taken within hours after conception, the PEBC will prevent the progesterone from reaching the egg, and the egg from attaching to the uterine lining. With the process interrupted, the fertilized egg will be flushed out of the system, just as an unfertilized egg would be. That is why we prefer to call it a post-effect birth control pill, rather than an abortion pill."

"But it is, in fact, an abortion pill, is it not?"

"In that it aborts a process already under way, yes, it is an abortion pill."

"Tell me, Dr. Kasabian, if Humaricare is successful, how lucrative might this be?"

Dr. Kasabian shook her head. "I don't really know," she said. "I'm a medical research specialist, not an accountant."

"But you have attended meetings, prepared reports and read documents. Surely you have some estimate?"

"I would think tens of billions of dollars," she said. "Beyond that I couldn't say."

"Then, laying aside the medical, ethical, and moral questions, and looking at it only from a business perspective . . . we are talking about something that could equal the gross national product of some nations. Am I right?"

"Perhaps," Dr. Kasabian agreed. "As I said, I am an M.D., not an MBA."

"It is safe to say that there's a lot riding on this, isn't it? Money, reputations, careers?"

"Yes, of course."

"What about the investors in this project? Do they receive periodic reports as to the progress you're making?"

"Yes."

"Who prepares these reports?"

"We all have a hand in it. Data is gathered from all the departments, but the final draft is put together by Dr. Corrigan."

"Was Dr. Corrigan in the process of preparing such a report just before Dr. Shaw was killed?"

"Yes."

"On the whole, what would you say was the tone of that report?"

"It was a very favorable report," Dr. Kasabian said.

Stone started walking toward the jury box. "And was this favorable report an accurate representation of your progress?"

"Yes, I would say so. We had just made a couple of significant breakthroughs. Everyone was excited by that."

When Stone heard Dr. Kasabian say that the report was accurate, he stopped in mid-stride and turned back toward her with a surprised expression on his face.

"I beg your pardon, Doctor? Did you say the report was accurate?"

"Yes, very accurate. The report went into some detail, charting several successful test sequences. We feel that we are only a few months away from filing an application to the FDA for its eventual use."

Stone walked back to the witness chair. It was obvious to everyone in the court that this wasn't the answer he was expecting.

"Excuse me, Doctor, but wasn't there some trouble with something called 'batch 9384'?"

"Yes there was, but it was nothing serious. We had a simple procedural error in the lab, which gave us some faulty support data. But that was a procedural error only. As soon as we got that cleared up, the test sequence was rerun and it emerged well within the prescribed parameters."

Stone stood there for a long moment, looking at Dr. Kasabian as if he couldn't believe what he was hearing. Then he walked over to the table and looked through several papers, finally holding one up.

"Doctor, you do remember something called a Tairge file, don't you?"

"Yes, of course I do."

"What is the Tairge file?"

"It was a file Dr. Shaw and I used to communicate with each other."

"A secret file?"

"It was a locked file, yes."

"By locked file, do you mean that no one else could get into it?"

"Not unless they knew the password."

"Which was Tairge?"

"Yes."

"Why was it necessary for you and Dr. Shaw to maintain a secret file?"

"Well, you would have to have known Gary Shaw. He was a brilliant man, but a little paranoid."

"Paranoid?"

"He tended to see schemes and plots in everything. Sometimes his paranoia could be quite disruptive. Finally Dr. Corrigan came up with an idea. He suggested that I establish a secret file to be used only by Gary and me. That way Gary could get things off his chest anytime he wanted, without fear of censorship, and without disrupting the entire lab."

Stone ran his hand across the top of his head. "Dr. Kasabian, are you telling me that this secret file you and Dr. Shaw maintained was begun at the suggestion of Dr. Corrigan?"

"Yes. Dr. Corrigan thought it would be good therapy for Dr. Shaw."

"Did Dr. Shaw know that Dr. Corrigan suggested the file?"

"Oh, heavens no. Gary would never have gone along with it if he had known it was Dr. Corrigan's idea. In fact, Dr. Shaw didn't even know that Dr. Corrigan knew about it. That way, he was able to say anything he wanted, no matter how outrageous it might be. And sometimes he could come up with some pretty outrageous ideas."

"Did Dr. Corrigan have access to this file?"

"No. He was very good about that. I offered to share the information with him, but he thought it would be better to let Gary rant and rave all he wanted."

"I see," Stone said. He looked at the paper in front of him. "I'd like to read something to you, Dr. Kasabian. Tell me if you recognize it."

Stone put on his glasses, then began to read in a monotone voice from the paper he was holding:

"Hi, L, have you got a minute? I want to ask you something."

"Sure, what?"

"You're closer to D than I am. Does he have a wild hair up his ass today or is it just me?"

"It isn't just you. He's very nervous about the status report he's giving to the shareholders next week."

"I don't blame him. When they find out what happened to batch 9384, they're going to be pretty upset. They might even pull the plug."

"Oh, I hope not. If they pull the plug, that will be the end of everything around here. We'll be out of a job!"

"Not to worry, my dear, D might not find as cushy a spot as he has now, but he'll land on his feet somewhere. We all will. Don't forget, I've got that offer from Chicago. If you'd like me to, I'll see that you get an interview with them too."

"Thanks, but I'd rather stay here. Wouldn't you like to see us complete our work?"

"Of course. If I didn't feel that way, I

would've already taken the Chicago position. But I don't see how we can continue here if our funding isn't renewed, and that's not likely to happen when they find out how far away we really are. Has D prepared the report yet?"

"Yes."

"Have you read it?"

"Yes."

"I'd sure like to see what he has to say."

"It's in the Admin file. I don't think he's locked it, but he may have. I'm not sure D would want you to read it, though."

"Why not?"

"I just think he would rather you not read it."

"Now you've really got me curious. I think I'll just drop out for a few minutes and take a look at it."

"I'm back! I can see why he wouldn't want me to read it. Can you believe that phony piece of shit D is submitting? He's using false data for the consequence 9384 batch! Did you know he was going to do this?"

"Yes. He told me what he was going to do."

"He sure as hell didn't say anything to me about it."

"He knew you would disapprove."

"You're damn right I disapprove. What about you, L? Didn't you tell him he was knowingly submitting faulty data?"

"I was more subtle with it, but I did remind him of the faulty test run with 9384."

"What did he say?"

"He said the misinformation was only a matter of timing and was of no consequence to the final report anyway. He's going to issue a correction in a few weeks. He'll tell them that the 9384 charts are based upon an honest error made in the analysis recording. By that time the new funding will already be locked in and we can carry on our work."

"This isn't right, L. If they can't trust him with that, how can they trust him with anything? He's going to cause the whole thing to blow up right in our faces. I'm going to have a talk with him."

"I don't think you should."

"Why not?"

"Because his mind is pretty well made up."

"Then I'm going to do everything in my power to unmake it."

Stone removed his glasses and lay them on the table, then looked over at Dr. Kasabian. "Is that an accurate reading, Doctor?"

"Yes, I think so."

"Well, according to this, you weren't all that close to success, were you? In fact you were so far away from it that Dr. Shaw suggested that the truth would cause the plug to be pulled."

"Dr. Shaw was an alarmist."

"Dr. Kasabian, did you or did you not come to me with this file?" Stone asked.

"Yes, I brought it to you."

"And did you or did you not suggest that Humaricare was not as close to success as Dr. Corrigan was leading everyone to believe?"

"Yes, I said that too."

"Then why are you changing your story now?"

"I am not changing my story, Mr. Stone. Dr. Corrigan is a man of unbridled optimism and confidence. One would have to be that way in order to hold the position he holds. If you listen to him, we could start manufacturing the pills tomorrow. Dr. Shaw, on the other hand, was the consummate pessimist. He believed failure was just around the corner. I consider myself the pragmatist. We aren't ready to start manufacturing the pills tomorrow, but Dr. Corrigan has a much better grasp of where we are than did Dr. Shaw."

Stone rubbed his hand across his cheek as if wiping this line of questioning away.

"Very well, Dr. Kasabian, let's go on to something else. Earlier in this trial you heard a cassette tape being played from Dr. Corrigan's answering machine, did you not?"

"Yes."

"I ask you now if that was your voice on the tape, requesting Dr. Corrigan to please speak with Dr. Shaw?"

"Yes."

"Where were you when you made that call?"

"I was at home. I had just left Gary at the clinic."

"Why did you want Dr. Corrigan to speak with Dr. Shaw?"

"Well, as I said on the tape, Gary—that is, Dr. Shaw—was upset. I thought Dr. Corrigan might be able to calm him down."

"After your voice is heard on the tape, we heard the voice of Dr. Shaw, and the voice of Dr. Corrigan. Were those, in fact, their voices?"

"I believe so. It sounded like them."

"Did Dr. Corrigan go down to the clinic to see Dr. Shaw?"

"I don't know."

"Would you say there was bad blood between Dr. Shaw and Dr. Corrigan?"

"Bad blood? No, I don't think so. They were both brilliant and headstrong men who sometimes interpreted the same information differently. As I said, David was the optimist and Gary the pessimist. But all in all, I think the combination worked well together. They made a good team, keeping each other in check, so to speak."

"Would you say they were men who had a passionate belief in what they were doing?"

"Yes."

"Passionate personalities?"

"Yes."

"Volatile?"

"Objection, Your Honor, calls for a conclusion."

"I'm asking for an observation, Your Honor. She worked with these men on a daily basis. Surely she had made some observation of their personalities."

"Overruled. Witness may answer the question."

"I would say they were passionate and dedicated men. I wouldn't say they were volatile," Dr. Kasabian replied.

"But weren't you concerned enough about it to believe that Dr. Corrigan might have killed Dr. Shaw?"

"No."

"No? Then why did you bring all this information to us, Dr. Kasabian?"

"Because I believed then, as I do now, that David is innocent. And I believed that the truth would help him prove his innocence."

"I have no further questions of this witness, Your Honor," Stone said disgustedly.

Moore looked up from the defense table, smiling broadly.

"Dr. Kasabian, much has been made about the report Dr. Corrigan submitted, giving a positive light to the research so far. In the so-called 'Tairge file,' Dr. Shaw suggests that it was false. Was it false?"

"There was some misleading information in it."

"By misleading information, are you talking about batch 9384?"

"Yes. Ironically, the test conclusion was accurate. The fault was in the procedure which produced the conclusion. It's a little like getting the right answer to a math problem, even though you have used the wrong formula. The bottom line was the same, and Dr. Corrigan felt that going into detail to explain the faulty procedure would only complicate things. It was particularly important that we keep the enthusiastic support of the board of directors, because we were about to have our funding renewal reviewed."

"Did Dr. Shaw understand that?"

"At first Dr. Shaw believed that we could explain away the mistake and still keep the funding. I talked to him at some length, and I believe he was coming around to Dr. Corrigan's way of thinking. That's why I called Dr. Corrigan. And I'm sure that's why Dr. Shaw called as well."

"Objection, Your Honor. Witness has no way of knowing what Dr. Shaw's true reason for calling was."

"You are objecting to an answer given by your own witness, counselor?" Judge Heckemeyer said.

"When the witness is a Trojan horse, yes," Stone replied.

"Now I object, Your Honor," Moore said.

"Both objections are sustained. You will strike the answer as to why Dr. Shaw may have called. And, Mr. Stone, there will be no more references to Trojan horses."

"No more questions, Your Honor," Moore said.

"Redirect, Mr. Stone?"

Stone let Dr. Kasabian sit on the witness chair for a long, long moment. He stared at her but said nothing. She began to grow noticeably nervous.

"Mr. Stone?" Heckemeyer asked again.

"No redirect, Your Honor."

"What do we do now?" Claire whispered to Stone when he returned to the prosecution table.

"I don't know," Stone replied. "But I'm afraid we've been had."

"Prosecution may call its next witness," Judge Heckemeyer said.

Stone hesitated for another moment.

"Do you have another witness?" the judge asked.

Stone stood. "I, uh . . . Your Honor, I would like to request a recess until tomorrow morning."

"Objection, Your Honor!" Moore said, standing quickly. "It should be very clear by now that the prosecution has no more witnesses and no case. They were pinning everything on Dr. Kasabian's testimony, having obviously totally misunderstood what she was telling them all along. Now he is trying to delay the inevitable. The truth is, he could wait until tomorrow morning, next week, or next month, and the facts aren't going to change. They have not been able to make their case."

"Mr. Stone, why do you want the recess? What, specifically, are you looking for?"

"I want to compare the testimony of this witness with statements she made during the pretrial interviews. I believe we may have some perjured testimony."

The judge sighed and stroked his chin. "Mr. Stone, we are trying a murder case here, not perjury. The State cannot be expected to compensate for your faulty preparation. If you have any more witnesses or evidence, then I suggest you bring them forth now. Otherwise, rest your case."

"But, Your Honor—"

"Rest your case, sir."

Stone looked over at Dr. Corrigan. The smug smile on his face told him that the man was as guilty as sin. He was guilty of murder, and he was going to get away with it because there was no ammunition left in the prosecution's arsenal.

"Prosecution rests, Your Honor," Stone said with a surrendering sigh.

"Your Honor, request a directed verdict!" Moore said, jumping up quickly. "Prosecution has failed to make its case."

Judge Heckemeyer stroked his chin again. "I'm going to take the recommendation of the defense for a directed verdict under advisement," he said. "Court is recessed until nine o'clock tomorrow morning, at which time I will give my decision."

Office of the District Attorney

Wentworth leaned back in his chair and tapped a pen against his palm. He looked across his desk at Ben Stone and Claire Kincaid.

Stone chuckled.

"Something funny?" Wentworth asked.

"I was just thinking of the way Kasabian set us up," he said. "I haven't been had like that since the last time my uncle asked me to pull on his finger."

Wentworth laughed.

"What do you mean the last time your uncle had you pull on his finger?" Claire asked.

"I would pull and he would fart," Stone said. He and Wentworth laughed again. "I fell for it every time."

"I don't understand," Claire said, confused by their laughter.

"Maybe it's a little boy thing," Wentworth suggested.

"Male bonding?"

"In a manner of speaking, I suppose," Stone said, still laughing.

"Well, all I can say is, I don't see how you two can sit there laughing when this case has come down around our ears."

"What would you have us do, Claire?" Stone asked.

"I don't know. But I sure can't sit around and laugh about it. I guess the reason I'm taking it so hard is because it's all my fault," Claire answered. "I was so anxious to prosecute."

"Don't play the martyr, Claire," Wentworth said. "Nothing is prosecuted out of this office unless I say it is."

"What do you think, Adam? Will Heckemeyer give Moore a directed verdict?" Stone asked.

"No," Wentworth answered. He sighed. "Although it might be more merciful if he would. I think he's going to make us play it out."

"Ben, is there anything we can do?" Claire asked.

"Do you play bridge, Claire?"

"Bridge? Not often, but I have played it. Why do you ask?"

"You know what it's like when your opponent bids a grand slam and holds all the trumps? You have to just sit there and watch him take all your high cards, knowing there's absolutely nothing you can do about it."

"Yes, I think I'm beginning to see what you mean. We're going to be doing that tomorrow, aren't we?"

"Yep," Stone replied. "Every piece of evidence we've introduced, and all the testimony, is going to be disassembled, right before our eyes."

"I don't want to watch."

"Oh, but you should," Wentworth said. "It will be a good lesson for you."

"If you say so," Claire replied. "But I've never considered humiliation to be a particularly good learning experience."

Chapter
Twelve

Spectrum

"Talk about your proverbial bombshell," Lee said. "One went off today in the Abortion Pill Murder case, in the form of Dr. Linda Kasabian, the prosecution's star witness. If her testimony was supposed to be a rocket, one might say she fizzled out on the launch pad. I am Brook Lee and you are watching Spectrum. My guests, as they have been every night since the trial began, are Mason Alexander from the pro-choice side of the abortion issue, and Dexter Keene from the pro-life side.

"Gentlemen, your comments."

"I, for one, will be very surprised if the judge even allows the trial to continue tomorrow," Mason Alexander said. "The prosecution's case depended entirely upon testimony from Dr. Kasabian, and that testi-

mony, if anything, strengthened the case for the Defense."

"Mr. Keene, do you agree?"

"As much as I dislike being on the same side as my worthy adversary, I have to say that I agree with him. There is no case for the prosecution. Dr. Kasabian has completely destroyed it with her testimony."

"The prosecutor today, called Dr. Kasabian a Trojan horse. Do you believe she is? Mr. Alexander?"

"I think that is sour grapes on the part of the prosecutor. They prepared their case poorly and they couldn't carry it off. It's as simple as that."

"Mr. Keene?"

"I think she may have been a plant," Keene said. *"But I don't think she did it to destroy the case for the prosecution. I think she did it to bring about a mistrial. There is a large and monied group of people who want this case over with . . . preferably without any convictions."*

"Now, wait a minute," Alexander said. *"Where does that piece of intelligence come from?"*

"Think about it," Keene said. *"When the prosecutor asked Dr. Kasabian how much money there was to be made from the successful development of the abortion pill, she answered in the tens of billions. Baby murder can be a very profitable exercise."*

"Oh, for heaven's sake, Keene. People like you see a conspiracy behind every corner. There is no conspiracy here."

"Then what is it?"

"It is no more than incredibly bad preparation on the part of the prosecution, that's all."

"Maybe you—"

That was as far as Dexter Keene got before Claire clicked the TV off. If there was anything she didn't need right now, it was listening to some TV pundit tell the world how incredibly poor her preparation had been.

Ben was right. She would have been better off had she never watched the first one of these ridiculous shows. She searched through the channels until she found a stand-up comedienne. She stayed there. She could use a laugh or two tonight. Tomorrow wasn't going to be fun.

Superior Court, the next day

"After due consideration of the defense's request that I issue a directed verdict, I have decided it would not fully serve justice for me to do so. Therefore, we will try the issue to its conclusion. Mr. Moore, are you ready to present your case?"

"I am, Your Honor."

"Call your first witness."

"Your Honor, Defense calls Dr. Victor Trailins."

When Trailins was on the stand, Moore began: "Dr. Trailins, how long have you been working on the PEBC project?"

"For two years."

"You have heard Dr. Kasabian testify that it is her belief that you are very close to success on the PEBC project?"

"Yes, sir."

"Do you agree with her assessment?"

"Absolutely. We are very close."

"Upon what do you base that observation?"

"We have been running a series of tests with the latest models, and every one has been successful. The concept is now totally proved . . . it is just a matter of selecting which is the best. If this were thirty years ago, I'm sure the product would already be on the market."

"Really? You believe you're that close?"

"Yes."

"Did Dr. Shaw share that optimism?"

"I would say Dr. Shaw was what you call cautiously optimistic. Like the rest of us, he thought we were on the right track. He didn't like to move forward too rapidly, though. He wanted to be absolutely certain of every test. That's why we had to completely rerun the batch 9384 sequence even though the first one proved out after the procedural error was corrected."

"Dr. Trailins, did you read the report Dr.

Corrigan submitted to the Humaricare board of directors?''

"Yes, sir, I read it.''

"What do you think about it?''

"It's a good report.''

"Accurate?''

"Yes, sir.''

"What about the information pertaining to batch 9384?''

"The results were accurate . . . the justification table in the report was incomplete.''

"Did Dr. Shaw say anything to you about that?''

"He said he thought we should hold up the report until the new figures were proved out.''

"Did you agree with him?''

"Not really. If the report had been going to another lab, or a specialist, then the justification table would have meant something. This report was going to a bunch of businessmen. I don't think the justification table meant anything to them.''

"Did the figures lie?''

"No. The figures weren't false, they were just incomplete. And actually, an addendum was already being prepared with the updated tables. Gary was just such a stickler that he wanted to wait for that, that's all.''

"Dr. Trailins, was there bad blood between Dr. Shaw and Dr. Corrigan?''

"No, I don't think so." Trailins chuckled. "Both men had egos so big they could hardly get them through the door. But I wouldn't say there was bad blood, no."

"Thank you, Doctor, no further questions."

Ben Stone rose from the prosecutor's table and approached the witness. "Dr. Trailins," he said. "Was there a pecking order within the clinic?"

"What do you mean?"

"I mean if Dr. Corrigan was gone and a decision had to be made right away, who would you go to? Would it have been Dr. Shaw?"

"Yes, I suppose so."

"Who would have been next?"

"Dr. Kasabian."

"And then who?"

"Well, I don't know. I don't think there was ever a time when all three of them were gone."

"Oh, come now, Dr. Trailins. You're being modest, aren't you? Isn't it true that you have now moved up in the pecking order? Aren't you now one of the top three?"

"Yes, I suppose so. But I don't know what you're getting at."

"That's what I'd like to know, Your Honor," Moore said. "Where is Mr. Stone going with this?"

"Your Honor, Defense has introduced Dr. Trailins as a disinterested witness. I am merely trying to establish the fact that he is not all that disinterested."

"You may continue."

"Dr. Trailins, if Humaricare successfully introduces the PEBC, would you be personally rewarded in any way?"

"There is a bonus for all of us who worked on the project," Trailins said.

"What would your share of that bonus be?"

"I'm not sure."

"Let me remind you. Before Dr. Shaw was killed, the position you occupied would have netted you a bonus of one quarter of a million dollars. In your new position, your bonus would be something over a million. That gives you quite a vested interest in the success of the project, doesn't it?"

"Objection, Your Honor. What does that have to do with anything?"

"Sustained. Make your point, counselor."

"Withdraw the question," Stone said, sitting down.

After Trailins, Moore interviewed two other research doctors, both of whom confirmed Trailins's testimony that they were very close to success. He did not put Corrigan on the stand.

"Defense rests, Your Honor," he said when the last witness finished.

"Are you ready for your summation, Mr. Moore?"

"I am, Your Honor."

"Please proceed."

Thurman Moore walked over to address the jury.

"Ladies and gentlemen of the jury, this trial has been one with national . . . no, make that international exposure. Before the first piece of evidence was presented, before the first witness was heard, pundits were trying this on talk shows on TV and radio." He walked back over to the table and picked up a stack of national news magazines.

"You have been in a news blackout for the duration of the trial, and rightly so, for everyone else has made the decision for you. Here is a cover story . . . I won't identify the magazines nor tell you anything of the content. The titles and the cover photos will speak for themselves."

He held a magazine out. "This one says 'Abortion Pill Murder.' Here's one, 'Abortion Means Big Bucks.' And this one says, simply, 'Abortion Murder.' " He tossed them back on the table. "As you can see, they all played up the abortion angle because that's what has made this such a high-profile case.

"But you, ladies and gentlemen of the jury, have sat here patiently, weighing the evidence, listening to the testimony, and formulating your own opinion, an opinion, I might add, based upon the facts of the case, and not upon the hyperbole.

"Yesterday, you heard me ask the judge for a directed verdict. I didn't do that to shortchange the system. It was not my intention to exclude you from this wonderful process of justice which we enjoy. I did it because I believed that the prosecution fell so far short of making its case that there was no need to waste any more of your time. I might say that these requests are routinely made . . . and just as routinely dismissed on the spot. After considering it overnight, Judge Heckemeyer decided to allow the case to go to the jury, so now, ladies and gentlemen, the decision is up to you."

He pointed to the defendant. "This man's future is in your hands. Years of study, dedication, and work are yours to endorse or destroy. The responsibility is awesome. Fortunately, your decision-making need not be difficult.

"You have heard Dr. Corrigan's peers testify that Dr. Corrigan is near the culmination of the most impressive work of his life. And, in Prosecution's own words, money, power, and prestige lie just before him.

"Does it seem reasonable to you that a man of Dr. Corrigan's intelligence would destroy all that in a move as irrational as the killing of one of his colleagues?

"Prosecution would have you believe this, but

they have no evidence to support their claim. They never found the gun that killed Dr. Shaw, but they did find the empty shell casing which the lab matched with the fatal bullet. And where did they find it? They found it in the apartment of Paul Alfusco, a man who confessed to breaking in on that fatal night, and a man who has a history of violent demonstration, as evidenced by the bomb he planted in the ROTC building of Kensington College in 1968. Incredibly, Paul Alfusco, a man who admits breaking into the building, a man who admits to having a violent past, and the man who was in possession of the expended shell casing that killed Dr. Shaw, was never even a serious suspect in this case.

"Instead, Prosecution based their entire case on the pretrial testimony they received from Dr. Linda Kasabian. When Dr. Kasabian's testimony from the witness stand failed to support their case, the prosecutor called her a Trojan horse, suggesting that she had, somehow, wormed her way into the prosecutor's camp so she could turn against them. But the truth is, Dr. Kasabian did not change one word of her testimony. What she said on the witness stand is exactly what she told them in pretrial statements. The problem is, they completely misunderstood her earlier testimony.

"I told you in my opening statement that, in

order to get a verdict of guilty, Prosecution had to prove, beyond any reasonable doubt, that Dr. Corrigan murdered Dr. Shaw. Well, ladies and gentlemen of the jury, Prosecution has fallen so far short of that mark that I almost hesitate to point it out to you, lest I be accused of overkill.

"Dr. Shaw's murder was a terrible tragedy, ladies and gentlemen. He was a brilliant researcher who, as Dr. Corrigan himself pointed out in a pretrial television interview, might well have discovered the cure to cancer, or AIDS, or one of a dozen other terrible maladies. Do not compound that tragedy with another, just as great. Do not interrupt the career of a brilliant, dedicated, and innocent man.

"I ask you to find Dr. David Corrigan not guilty."

Ben Stone waited until Moore sat down before he stood up.

"The defense attorney is wrong when he says that we have no physical evidence that points to the guilt of David Corrigan. We don't live in a vacuum, ladies and gentlemen, and no matter how hard someone may try to cover their tracks, there is always something left as a trail. Like the trackers in the days of the old West, it is merely a matter of knowing where to look. If you'll come along with me, I will take you, step by step, along the trail that will lead us to the inescapable conclusion that David Corrigan killed Gary Shaw.

"The trail begins with the telephone calls. We know the calls were made, because we have the cassette tape from the answering machine. You heard Dr. Kasabian testify that she made that telephone call from her home at ten-thirty that evening. You also heard her say that Dr. Shaw was still at the office, and then we heard Dr. Shaw's voice answering. We have a further verification of that conversation from a witness who was in the clinic at the time of the call, listening from the hall just outside Dr. Shaw's office.

"Did Dr. Corrigan go down to the clinic to speak with Dr. Shaw? Well, let's look at it reasonably. Dr. Shaw was Dr. Corrigan's second-in-command. A reasonable person, in a position as responsible as that held by Dr. Corrigan, would be expected to answer a request from his second-in-command, when the request is made in a tone of voice as urgent and as agitated as the tone of voice used by Dr. Shaw. You don't have to take my word for how his voice sounded. You heard the tape, you heard his words and their timbre. Wouldn't you answer such a request?

"But it isn't just reason which suggests that Dr. Corrigan did, in fact, go down to the clinic. Consider this. You heard Jerry Talbot testify that when he went down to leave his poster, the front door was unlocked. He walked in through the front door. Hearing someone from back in the office, he moved quietly down the hall to see who it was. That was when he saw Dr. Shaw, who was even then on the phone, speaking with Dr. Corrigan. We know he was speaking with Dr. Corrigan, because Talbot hear him say, quite clearly, 'You know damn well what's wrong. We have to talk, and we have to talk now.' What he heard matches up with what was on the tape, though Mr. Talbot's version does go a few words beyond what we heard.

"Talbot then sneaked back into the front lobby, left his poster on the wall, and left.

"You may recall that I asked him if he locked the door as he left and his reply was that he did not lock the door, because the door could only be locked by someone who had a key.

"However, we then heard testimony from Paul Alfusco, telling us that when he came to the clinic later that same night, he had to break out the front window in order to gain entry, because the door was locked. Now, what does that tell us? That tells us that someone, with a key to the door, was there between the time Jerry Talbot left, and the time Paul Alfusco arrived. Jerry Talbot believes he left somewhere between ten-thirty and eleven. Paul Alfusco believes he was there at around midnight. Who was there between eleven and midnight?

"Well, since Dr. Shaw was so adamant in demanding that Dr. Corrigan come to speak with him, can't we make the reasonable assumption that it was he who came between the hours of eleven and midnight?

"When Alfusco went back to Dr. Shaw's office at around midnight, he found Shaw dead. Alfusco did not find the pistol, but he did find the empty cartridge, which he picked up and put in his pocket. He then returned to the lobby, where he opened the file cabinets and scattered the papers around to, as he says, further confuse the issue.

"Alfusco says he did nothing to the computers, even though the computers were purged . . . all, that is, except the one which was conveniently off-line. Now, why would Alfusco admit to breaking in the window and admit to scattering the files, but not admit to purging the computers? The answer is simple. He didn't purge the computers. Whoever murdered Dr. Shaw purged the computers.

"The trail that we have just followed, points clearly to David Corrigan. We know he received a telephone call from Gary Shaw somewhere between ten-thirty and eleven. We believe he then went down to see him. There, they got into an argument. As a result of or possibly an extension of that argument, David Corrigan went into his office and took out a nine millimeter pistol from his desk. We know that he owns a nine millimeter pistol, because he has a registration certificate for that kind of gun. Armed, David then returned to Shaw's office and shot him. After that, he purged the computers, though I now believe that he did so knowing full well that one was off-line and thus would not be affected. Finally, he locked the door and left. That is why the door was locked when Alfusco arrived.

"Doesn't that all seem reasonable to you? I have to tell you, I didn't plan to guide you through the scenario like this. I thought we would have a witness whose testimony would make it all crystal clear to you without the necessity of a step-by-step guidance. Dr. Linda Kasabian was to have been that star witness. I think it is important that you know that we didn't seek her out. Oh no, she came to us. She was really quite wonderful, ladies and gentlemen, searching her soul for the right thing to do. Should she share information with us that would most certainly implicate Dr. Corrigan in this murder, or was her loyalty to him more important?

"Though she dissembled on the witness stand, I have to tell you that in our many pretrial discussions, she was most compelling. She told how Dr. Corrigan was so driven by the money, power, and prestige he had already achieved as head of the PEBC project, that he would do anything to keep the funding and the research going. Anything to include lying, and murder.

"Now, why would she do such a thing? Why would she introduce evidence and testimony that points to Dr. Corrigan's guilt . . . then get on the witness stand and do everything she can to undermine the very evidence and testimony she had provided in the first place?

"I think I know the answer to that. Though we did not know it when we began this trial, we now know that Dr. Linda Kasabian and Dr. David Corrigan are more than colleagues in the workplace. They are lovers as well, and women have taken risks for their men since the beginning of time. That is a bit romantic, I suppose. You might even say it is courageous, though it is terribly misplaced courage. Brilliant? Yes, in the same way that evil genius is often brilliant.

"How did she do it?

"The answer to that, ladies and gentlemen, is simple. But then, most brilliant things are simple.

"Dr. Kasabian and Dr. Corrigan are well aware, as I am sure you are, of the law of double jeopardy. Once found innocent of a crime, a person cannot be tried again. By stacking the evidence in the way that she did, Dr. Kasabian was actually setting a very clever trap. She allowed us to build our case around her pretrial testimony. Then, once she had us vulnerable, all she had to do was pull the lever and the trap would slam shut.

"I stand before you now, confessing my failure to you. Sacrificing my ego and self-esteem to you like a trapped beaver will sacrifice his own foot, gnawing it off to escape.

"Look at the defendant, ladies and gentlemen," Stone invited, pointing toward the defense table and Dr. Corrigan. "Look at that smug expression on his face. He thinks he has beaten the system . . . and if he is found innocent, he *has* beaten the system. For once he gets out of our grasp, there will be nothing we can do.

"I'm going to be honest with you," Stone said, turning back to look at the jury with earnest eye contact. "I know I'm fighting an uphill battle. I am the lawyer of the people . . . I carry that responsibility on my shoulders. I represent the citizens of New York, and I have stumbled. But the same people who put in the part about double jeopardy also put in safeguards to protect the citizenry from the evildoers. Fortunately, I am not the State's last line of defense. You are.

"No matter how badly I may have done on this case, you are the final decision maker. Judge Heckemeyer realizes that, which is why he did not preempt your right to decide. You have it in your power to undo the evil that they have done. You can still hold Dr. Corrigan accountable for the murder of Gary Shaw. And if you do that, I guarantee you, I'll have an indictment against Dr. Kasabian for her part in this by the next day.''

Later, in the office of the District Attorney

"The jury is back," Wentworth said, hanging up the telephone. He stood up. "If you'd like, I'll go with you."

"Thanks, Adam, but I'm the one who screwed up. There's no sense in your taking any of the heat." He looked over at Claire and smiled. "You don't have to come either if you don't want to."

Claire shook her head. "I'm coming," she said. "Aren't you the one who told me about the lessons one can learn from humiliation?"

"I'd rather you call that humility."

"Well, where do you think the word humility comes from?" Claire replied.

Half an hour later the court was reassembled and the jury was brought back into the box.

"Ladies and gentlemen of the jury, have you reached a verdict?"

"We have, Your Honor," the foreman of the jury answered. The foreman was a woman, comfortable enough with her attractive looks that she made no effort to dye her graying her.

"Please hand the verdict to the bailiff."

The bailiff took a piece of paper from the woman, then walked over and handed it to the judge. Judge Heckemeyer looked at the paper for a moment, then handed it back. The bailiff returned the paper to the foreman.

"Please read the verdict," Judge Heckemeyer said.

"In the case of the State of New York verses David Corrigan, to the charge of murder in the second degree, we find the defendant . . . not guilty."

"Yeah!" Dr. Corrigan said, slamming his hand down on the table, then shaking hands with Thurman Moore.

"Look," Claire said. She pointed to Linda Kasabian, who made no effort to hide her joy. She hurried through the opening in the little railing that separated the front of the court from the gallery, then went to Dr. Corrigan. They embraced, then kissed, deeply.

"Would you say that is a little more than a congratulatory kiss?" Stone asked.

"I'd say so," Claire replied.

Both Corrigan and Kasabian looked over at the prosecutor's table and laughed.

"Better luck next time, Ben," Moore said, coming over to extend his hand. He laughed. "Oh, I forgot. There won't be a next time, will there?"

"Thurman, he is guilty as sin and you know it," Stone said.

"I really don't think he is, Ben. And what's more important, the jury didn't think so either. Now, if you'll excuse me, I've got to get back to the office. I have half a dozen calls waiting. And my rates have just gone up."

Stone looked over at Claire, then smiled at the hangdog look on her face.

"Cheer up, counselor," he said. "I'll tell you something my dad told me a long time ago. They can kill us, but they can't eat us."

"Thank you, Ben. That was very comforting," Claire said with a laugh.

"Now, what do you say we get out of here? I can't stand to look at them celebrating," Stone said.

"I'm with you," Claire agreed.

Chapter
Thirteen

One month later

Ben Stone looked up from his desk to see Lennie Briscoe standing at the door.

"Hello, Lennie, what's up?" he asked.

"We've got someone down at the station house I think you might want to talk to," he said.

"On the Fillmore case?"

"Uh-uh," Briscoe said. "The Corrigan case."

"Corrigan? David Corrigan."

"Yes."

Stone smiled and shook his head. "What are you doing messing around with that case, Lennie? You know it's closed, and there's not a damn thing we can do about it."

"Yeah, I know. I really think you ought to

come talk to her, though. Maybe you can come up with an idea of what to do."

"Talk to *her*?" Stone got up and walked over to get his coat from the rack. "Why is it I have a sick feeling about this? Please tell me the person you want me to talk to isn't Linda Kasabian."

"You guessed it."

"It is her? Damn. I wanted that person out of my life—forever. What does she want?"

"She wants to tell everything she knows," Briscoe said. "She says she's ready to sign a statement accusing David Corrigan of the murder."

"Claire?" Stone called to his assistant. She looked up from her desk. "You want to come with me?"

"Sure," Claire said. "Where are we going?"

"You don't want to know," Stone answered.

Dr. Kasabian's eyes were red-rimmed from crying, and she ground out her cigarette as Stone and Claire entered the interrogation room.

"I . . . I don't suppose you're too happy to see me," she said.

"You've got that right," Stone replied. "What do you want, Doctor?"

"I want to make up for what I did during the trial."

"It's too late for that."

"No, no it isn't. I'm willing to sign a sworn statement. And I am willing to testify, under oath, against David. He killed Gary Shaw, and he admitted it to me."

"Why the change of heart, Doctor?" Stone asked. "Why are you willing to do now what you wouldn't do before?"

"When he came by my house that night after killing Shaw, he was crazed with fear. He begged me to help him. I couldn't turn my back on him. Then the test results of batch 9384 gave me an idea. The final result of that test was accurate, but the procedure was flawed. To anyone who didn't know the entire history of the project, the flawed procedure would be enough to overturn the results. I figured we could do the same thing in this case."

"So you fed us misleading information, knowing we would base our case around that. Then, discrediting our procedure would discredit our conclusion, right, Doctor?" Stone asked.

"Yes."

"Why, Dr. Kasabian?" Claire asked. "Why did you do it?"

"I was in love with him. Then."

"I see. And you aren't in love with him now?" Claire asked.

"I hate him now. He's going to marry Judy

Singleton. Can you believe that? After all I've done for him, he throws me over for that cow-eyed tramp."

"Dr. Kasabian, what makes you think anyone would listen to your testimony now, even if we could reopen the trial?" Stone asked.

"I have more than just testimony this time," Kasabian said. "For openers, I have his gun. Ballistics will prove that it's the one that killed Gary."

"That would've helped, but even the gun wouldn't have been conclusive."

"I also have an audiotape."

"What?"

Kasabian opened her purse and took out an audio cassette. "Gary told me several weeks ago that he had begun taping every conversation he had with David. You see, there was more than a simple misunderstanding about the test results between them. David was the director, but Gary was actually the guiding genius of the entire project. It was his formula that was most promising. He felt that David wasn't acknowledging that, and he was afraid David was somehow going to steal his work. The taping was his way of protection."

"Wait a minute," Stone said. "Are you telling me you actually have an audiotape of the murder?"

"Yes. I went back that night and got the tape. Not even David knows that I have it."

"Get a tape player, Mike," Stone said.

Logan left the room, then returned a moment later with the recorder. Stone put the tape in and punched the play button.

"All right, Gary, what is it? What is so important you have to get me down here in the middle of the night?"

"I'm going to ask you one more time to give me the recognition I deserve for my role in the PEBC project."

"I do acknowledge you, for chrissake. I've told everyone how valuable you are."

"Don't patronize me, David. That's no more than you would say to Trailins or King, or any of the others."

"They're valuable too. We're a team, can't you see that?"

"We are a team . . . but you're the quarterback, is that it?"

"There can only be one quarterback."

"I want you to step down."

"What? You're talking like a madman. Why should I step down?"

"Because if you don't, I will. And if I leave here, David, my work leaves here with me. Do you think I couldn't find half a dozen other companies who wouldn't take me on in a minute?"

"Try and do that and I'll have you in court."

"Do you think I give a damn about that? The only thing that would do would be to bring PEBC to a complete halt. And you'd better believe that my testimony in court will spill the beans on everything I've done here . . . which, if you're honest with yourself, is about eighty percent."

"You wouldn't dare."

[Laughter] "I sort of have you now, don't I, David. You're either going to have to step down and recommend that I take your place . . . or you're going to see the entire project destroyed. And if the project is destroyed, your reputation will be as well. So what's it to be, David?"

"Neither."

"Neither? I'm sorry, that's not an acceptable answer. You're . . . what the hell? What are you doing with that gun?"

"I'm sorry, Gary. You leave me no choice. I will not see a lifetime of work destroyed by one madman."

"David, don't be silly, you—"

[sound of gunshot]

"You made me do it. Why? Why did you make me do it?"

That was the end of the tape.

"What about the Tairge file? The letters T-A?" Briscoe asked.

"I was in Gary's office when Alfusco broke the front window," she said. "It frightened me to death . . . I didn't know what was going on. I hid in Gary's bathroom and looked through a crack in the door when Alfusco came into the office. I saw him look around the room, pick up the shell casing, then leave. I waited for several minutes until I was sure he was gone.

"At the time, I had him confused. I knew he was one of the anti-abortion protesters, but I didn't know which one. The only name I knew was Talbot, so I got a piece of paper and wrote the letters T-A, then left it on Gary's desk. After that, I went to my computer and purged all the computers . . . though I made sure that at least one of them was off-line so we wouldn't really lose all the information. I figured that way the police would surely think it was the work of a protester, especially after the shootings that took place in Florida and Kansas.

"The more I thought about it, though, the less confidence I had in the scheme. I finally decided that we needed to come up with something else, and that was when I went to David with the idea that I would send up a smoke screen, get him tried, then acquitted. That way he would be protected for all time. He agreed to it, but that left me with the false clue I had planted about Talbot. So, in order to cover that, I just dreamed up the Tairge file. There was never any such thing. I put the file on the one computer that wasn't purged, then I waited for someone to discover it. Victor played right into my hands."

"And so did we, Doctor, so did we," Stone said.

"Yes, but I'm willing to come clean now."

"I'm sorry, Doctor. You did too good a job," Stone said. "There's nothing we can do about it."

"Maybe there is," Claire said.

"You have an idea?"

"Ben, let's go talk to Adam."

Adam Wentworth's office

Stone filled Wentworth in on their meeting with Dr. Kasabian, and on her willingness, eagerness even, to make a full statement about what happened.

"I figured there was nothing we could do about it," Stone said. "But Claire has come up with an idea that will work . . . if you'll go along with it."

"All right, Claire, let me hear it," Wentworth said, leaning back in his chair and folding his arms across his chest.

"Do you remember the Rodney King beating?" Claire asked.

"Christ, who the hell could forget that? We had to watch that tape over and over again for six months."

"Yes. Well, you're also aware that in the first trial, the policemen were all acquitted. Most Americans were appalled at what they thought was a miscarriage of justice, but they thought it was the end of it because of the principle of double jeopardy. Only it wasn't the end, was it?"

Wentworth leaned forward, resting his elbows on his desk. "They were tried in federal court for violating King's civil rights," he said.

Claire smiled. "Exactly."

"I'm not quite sure what you're getting at, Miss Kincaid. We have no jurisdiction in a federal court."

"No, we don't. But we do have a vested interest in seeing justice done. And if we screwed up, then we ought not to be too proud to exercise every option that is open to us . . . even if that option excludes us."

"You're saying you want to turn this over to the feds?"

"Yes."

"Then walk away?"

"Give them everything that we have, then walk away, yes," Claire said.

"What do you think, Ben?" Wentworth asked.

Ben chuckled. "Seems like I've spent an entire career fighting for turf with those guys," he said. "But I hate to see this smug son of a bitch get away with murder, and that's what's going to happen if we don't do this."

Wentworth drummed his fingers on the desk for a moment or two, then smiled. "Well, what the hell?" he said. "If the East can meet the West in Europe, then I don't see why we can't send out an overture to the feds. Get the material together, Ben. I've got a friend over in the Federal Building. I'll give him a call."

Stone and Claire left Wentworth's office. Stone was quiet for a long moment.

"Are you all right, Ben?" Claire asked.

"Yeah," he answered. "I'm all right."

"You're not upset about having to do it this way?"

"No. I guess that lesson you were talking about sunk in after all."

"What lesson?"

"The one in humility," Ben said.